GW00630684

The Connemara Five

Micheál Ó Conghaile

The Connemara Five

Translated from the Irish by
Úna Ní Chonchúir

ARLEN
HOUSE

The Connemara Five © Micheál Ó Conghaile 2006

The moral rights of the author have been asserted

First published in English by Arlen House in 2006

Arlen House
PO Box 222
Galway
Ireland
Phone/fax 086 8207617
arlenhouse@gmail.com

ISBN 1-903631-79-3, hardback
ISBN 1-903631-99-9, signed and numbered limited edition

Artwork: "Methosis" by Seán Ó Flaitheartha, courtesy of the artist
Typesetting: Arlen House
Printed by: Betaprint, Dublin

for

The Rossport Five

"As this is Connemara I don't know where to go",
from the song "Máire Rua" by Cóilín MacDonncha

A licence for the production of this play may be obtained, on payment of a fee, by application to:

Cló Iar-Chonnachta
Indreabhán
Conamara
Co na Gaillimhe
Éire
Phone + 353-91-593307
Fax + 353-91-593362
Email: moccic@eircom.net
www.cic.ie

The Connemara Five

LIST OF CHARACTERS

DANNY	In his early thirties
DARACH	Danny's brother, about ten years older
COLEMAN	Their father, 70, doddering slightly
CYNTHIA	Danny's girlfriend, a few years younger
MAGGIE	Neighbour, around 65

Location/Time   Contemporary Connemara

Act One

SCENE ONE

Sitting-room/kitchen in a house in contemporary Connemara. Stage left is an upstairs bedroom with the stairs centre-stage. This area is unlit except during the bedroom scenes. Back of stage right there is a large window through which the Connemara mountains can be seen in the distance. Next to the window is the door facing the 'street'. Back of stage also is a door leading to a bedroom and front stage left is a door leading to another bedroom. Front stage right is a range on which there is a kettle.

The scene opens with Coleman sitting on the chair nearest the range, reading a newspaper which bears the front-page headline 'RAPIST JAILED FOR 15 YEARS'. Darach is looking out the window. He is dressed-up with his hair freshly-washed and has his coat on. He is pacing up and down, impatiently. Looks at his watch. COLEMAN glances furtively at him. Then each man raises his head to look at the other and inadvertently catches his eye.

COLEMAN: You're making me nervous there. Walking over and back.

DARACH: Nervous! Sure you were always nervous.

COLEMAN: I *was not* always nervous. I've only been nervous for the last twenty-five years. (*Pause*). I was alright when I was born and you were born.

DARACH: It's far from alright you are now.

COLEMAN: You're making me more nervous than I usually am, the way you're carrying on. That's what I mean to say.

DARACH: Well then, say what you mean to say and don't be saying things you don't mean to say. That's what causes half of the trouble in this world, you know. (*Pause*). People saying things they don't mean to say.

COLEMAN: Listen now, *a mhac*, I'm too old to be taking orders from the likes of you. I can talk to myself if I feel like it.

DARACH: You're well used to it. (*Pause*). Anyways, sure you're only an auld bag of nerves, a bag of nerves wired together –

COLEMAN: Connected up to you. (*Turns newspaper upside-down*).

DARACH: Connected up to me, unfortunately … but there's worse than you in it … Take that little fucker who never comes home on time. (*Looks at his watch*). I'll have missed half the match.

COLEMAN: And what are you waiting for?

DARACH: For you.

COLEMAN: I'm not going to go watching that stupid soccer.

DARACH (*Firmly*): Look it now, auld man! Don't be trying to rise me.

COLEMAN: You can feck off now for yourself. I'll not be keeping you. Danny'll be home now any second. I'll be grand here by myself.

DARACH: You will, you know; you'll be grand out. (*Pause*). Till you start drinking water out of a Wellie again, that is. (*Teasing laugh*). I wouldn't mind if you had a decent drink out of it. (*Pause. Angering again*). I don't know what the fucks wrong with him these days. He's no sooner in than he's gone out again – he's like an auld hen.

COLEMAN: I can't read my paper in peace with you.

DARACH: It'd be hard for you (*looks at him*) when you have it upside-down … (DARACH *takes the paper out of his hand, and turns it the right way about. Hands the paper back, open as if it were being read*). You might have some chance of reading it if you turned it that way. (*Pause*) Either that or you'll have to turn yourself upside down and put your head down where your feet are and your feet up on your head.

COLEMAN: You mean, I'll have to stand on my head with my two hands, is that what you mean to say?

DARACH: That's exactly what I mean to say. Stand on your brains.

COLEMAN: Or sit on them like you do!

DARACH (*Annoyed*): Look it now, Coleman, you're the one with the funny head, *a mhac*, not me. I wasn't reading the paper upside-down.

COLEMAN: Upside-down my arse … I was looking for the answers to the quiz and you have to turn the paper upside-down to read them. (*Turns the paper upside-down again cockily and starts scanning it*). I can't find the page now; you've put me off.

DARACH: Read it whatever way you like. Read it sideways if it makes you happy; turn sideways yourself for all I care.

COLEMAN: Look it, *a mhac*, I don't know what's got into you but don't be taking it out on me. Go on down to the pub if that's where you're going. I'll be grand here by myself.

DARACH: You will, yeah right. Sure you might fall into the range.

COLEMAN: … Into the range …

DARACH (*Sarcastically*): Or into the telly.

COLEMAN: Ah but there's plenty of people in the telly already … and anyways, it's turned off. And I'll leave it turned off until Danny comes in.

DARACH: The likes of you would nearly fall up the chimney.

COLEMAN: Up the chimney. When was the last time you saw a fella falling up the chimney. How could you fall up the chimney … unless you turned the house upside-down … You're losing it Darach, *a mhac* – losing it.

DARACH: If I am, I'm not the only one.

COLEMAN: There'll be no falling up anywhere, *muis*. (*Pause*). Unless the moon pulls me up. The moon can pull things you know – lunar pull I think they call it.

DARACH: Oh, it can, yeah, right.

COLEMAN: But sure, there's no moon tonight, so there isn't. It's as black as a tinker's soul out there. (*Pause*).

DARACH: The only lunar pull I know of is the looner inside your head – and he's there day and night.

COLEMAN: Ha?

DARACH: Nothing! (*Pacing the room*).

COLEMAN (*To himself*): A fella could fall down a chimney, right enough. He could, you know. That'd be natural enough, except that he'd have to be up on top of it in the first place ... I'd say. (*Pause. Looks at Darach*). And I'm not going up on top of any chimney tonight. The auld vertigo. I was never one for heights, anyways.

DARACH: Heights. Wouldn't you be some sight up on top of a chimney, like an old grey crow. (*Pause. To himself*). You'd make a fine lightening conductor.

COLEMAN: Ha?

DARACH: Ha? Ha?

COLEMAN: I said ha? Did you mention thunder? (*Sits up in the chair, slightly vexed*). If you did, don't mention it again.

DARACH: I was talking to myself. I wasn't talking to you.

COLEMAN: Oh, talking to yourself! (*Laughs*). So I'm not the only who goes around talking to himself?

DARACH: Look it. (*Cranky. Buttons up his coat*). I'm going out. Fall down and hit your head against the range if you like, or against the floor ... mind you, the range is harder. Maybe that's what you need – a good bang on the head. It might put your brains back where they're supposed to be.

COLEMAN: *Ara*, why would I hit my head against the range. I'll fall into it altogether. (*Pause*). All you'd see when you'd come home would be the tips of my toes sticking out of it ... But I suppose you wouldn't see that much itself if you were half as pissed as you were the other night. (DARACH *is angry. He stands at the door, hesitantly, unsure whether he should stay or go. He is outside Coleman's line of vision.* COLEMAN *starts reading his newspaper as though Darach had left.* DARACH *is still hesitating. He looks at the door, then looks over at Coleman and once again at the door. He decides to leave and is very annoyed. Heads for the door. Someone opens the door from the other side and the door misses Darach by inches.* DANNY *enters. He is wearing a coat under which he appears to be concealing a small package. He's holding a newspaper and there is another sticking out of an inside coat-pocket).*

DARACH: Where were you?

DANNY: Out!

DARACH: Out! I know bloody well you were out.

DANNY: And I suppose you know … bloody well … that I'm in now.

DARACH: Stop your fancy talking. I'm waiting here for the last hour for you.

DANNY: Well, an hour would hardly kill you … or what's your rush?

DARACH: There's a soccer match on, but of course, you'd know nothing about those things. And you're the one who's looking after the auld fella, not me, you know, and if you're not gonna look after him, throw him into the auld folk's home or send him over to Ballinasloe.

COLEMAN: You can't send me to Ballinasloe – we have our own Ballinasloe here now, you know, so we have.

DANNY: Off you go, so. Off you go – let me not be keeping you one second.

DARACH: I'll go in my own good time. (*Sits down for a minute, then leaves slowly*). I'll go and I'll come back to my own house in my own time. Whenever I feel like it. (*Standing in the doorway. Looks over at Coleman*). A Wellington! (*Laughs. Closes the door slowly behind him*).

DANNY: There's something eating him again tonight, whatever is making him so touchy.

COLEMAN: Mid-life crisis syndrome, maybe, or maybe his hormones are gone haywire. He's there at the door for the last hour like a cat that'd be watching a mouse. I told him to go on out. If I told him once, I told a thousand times.

DANNY: Well he's gone now and we might have a bit of peace, even if we'll never have the pounds. I brought the paper. (*Speaks good-humouredly and gives the newspaper to Coleman. About to unzip his anorak when something occurs to him. COLEMAN opens the newspaper. It's a broadsheet*).

COLEMAN: Did you not get me the small paper?

DANNY: I did, Dad, but I haven't read it myself yet. (*Takes out a tabloid newspaper carefully, barely opening his anorak, and hands it to him*). You'll have all the latest now about the races – all the scandal and the girls.

COLEMAN: About the jockeys.

DANNY: There's a great picture on page three today, Dad. It'd rise up your heart.

COLEMAN (*Opening the newspaper*): Ha-Ha! I'd say it'd rise up more than your heart – if Cynthia only heard you. I thought you said a minute ago you hadn't read the paper.

DANNY: I haven't. Not yet. I only checked page three for you before I bought it, to make sure it was worth buying. I looked at the pictures. I'm getting more like you by the day.

COLEMAN: Ha-Ha-Ha! (*Looking at the newspaper*). Where's page three? O Jesus! (*Reading. Brings the newspaper right up to his face*). 'In this Indian summer weather, sexy Tanya can't wait to wiggle her bum and drive out into the country for a picnic. She loves taking off her itsy-bitsy black bikini and sipping champagne under the shady trees while listening to the birds and the bees above her. But watch out for the insects, girl, you're got to be careful they don't join you for a little nibble'. Now what would you make of that! She might come to Connemara for her picnic. (*Turns the newspaper upside-down again. Brings it even closer to his eyes as if to focus more closely on it*).

DANNY: Are you trying to see both sides of her, is that it? I'll hang her in the bedroom for you tonight if you like. (*Pause*). Up above the Sacred Heart, where she'll have a little red light shining on her.

COLEMAN: Oh! Oh! If Maggie heard you! Never mind. I'll put her in under the pillow, where she'll be nearer to me.

DANNY: Whatever you think yourself.

COLEMAN (*Pause*): How is Cynthia anyways, or did you see her today?

DANNY: She's grand. (*Pause*). Grand, I think. I haven't seen her since Sunday. I think she's working late these days. (*Pause*). She didn't call while I was out, did she?

COLEMAN: She didn't, no. She won't be around tonight then?

DANNY: She won't, no. Today's Wednesday, isn't it? Are you going to bingo later on? (*Looks at his watch*).

COLEMAN: I am, of course. Anything that'll take me out of this hole for a few hours a week.

DANNY: You'd be right, I suppose.

COLEMAN: I might win the jackpot. (*Rubbing his hands together*). I'm feeling kind of lucky tonight so I am – lucky as a black cat.

DANNY: Or a bottle of whisky in the raffle. Will I give Maggie a ring?

COLEMAN: There's no need. Maggie will call round anyways.

DANNY: I suppose she will, the creature. I don't know what we'd do without Maggie. Will you be alright there on your own for a minute? I have to go and take a shower.

COLEMAN: Why wouldn't I? (*Pause*). A shower. (*Pause. Fiddles with the newspaper again*). Are you sure Cynthia isn't calling later on? (*Danny ignores the last question. He is at the top of the stairs by now. Takes a bunch of keys from his pocket and unlocks the door to his room. Opens the door, switches the light on and enters the room*).

Danny's room. An ordinary bedroom. Bed by the wall, and a stand-alone mirror in the centre of the room. A plastic curtain at the back of the room, where there is an off-stage shower. Pictures, etc, on the walls. A large photograph of Cynthia on the dressing-table.

DANNY *takes off his anorak and takes out a plastic bag which he had hidden under it. He sighs, as if tired and lost in thought. Sets the plastic bag on the bed. Sits down, turning his back to the audience. Takes the plastic bag in his hand. Takes some items of clothing out of the bag, but the audience cannot see them clearly. Handles the items of clothing carefully, affectionately. Examines them closely once more. Holds them up to his chest, lovingly.*

DANNY: Cynthia. Cynthia. (*Opens the bottom drawer and puts the clothes into the back of the drawer. Stands up*). What the hell is wrong with me? (*Pause. Sighs. Sits on a chair in front of the audience. Leans back, deep in thought*). Do you think, Cynthia … (*looking at the photograph*). Do you … Ara. Damn! (*He stands up. Takes off his jumper and shirt and throws them on the bed. Takes off his t-shirt. Sniffs it and throws it on the bed. Sits down and takes off his shoes and socks. Stands up. Stands still for a second. Takes off his trousers slowly, obviously thinking of something. Carefully folds the trousers and places them on the bed. Stands up in front of the mirror wearing only his underpants. Poses, slightly effeminately, without overdoing it. Walks towards the door which is closed, speaking as though he were addressing his father*). Do you think you'll survive much longer down there? (*Pause*). Fuck me! (*Pause*). Fuck me, Danny! What kind of thing is that to say? (*Asks the question as though surprised and ashamed at having asked it. Turns around and goes to the other side of the room towards the plastic shower curtain. Turns on the water which can be heard against the curtain. Crosses the room to get a clean towel. Returns to the shower and puts his hand in under the running water until he feels the water is hot. Growing increasingly impatient*). Don't say he's used all the fucking hot water as well. (*Pause. Hand still under the running water*). Thank Christ. (*Lights lower gradually.* DANNY *pulls down his underpants and steps in under the shower, hanging the towel outside as he does so. At the same time, the lights go up on the kitchen/sitting room where Coleman is reading the newspaper, or is fumbling with it at least. Some of the pages are strewn either side of him and he thumbs the pages clumsily*).

Sitting room/kitchen.

COLEMAN: There's fuck-all in this paper. They're not worth buying, you know. (*Pause*). Then again, when you don't buy them, you think you're missing out on something. (*Pause*). Some woman over in Louisiana who has twenty-eight cats ... for fuck's sake (*Reading*). 'They take turns sleeping with me in my bed'. That's grand till they start clawing at her in the middle of the night. Sure I suppose maybe she has them well trained. (*Reading. Pulls the newspaper in towards his face*). 'Since I was a child I was scared of mice and so began my lifelong relationship with cats ...' She must be 'cat' herself. Maybe her people came from Kilkenny. The mice won't come within an ass's roar of that one I'll tell you. (*Reading*). 'I have them all on a different diet'. She's a fucking ass herself. I'd say those cats wouldn't know a mouse if it bit them. What a load of rubbish. They should do a catscan on her head. (*Reading*). 'I hope to be reborn as a cat in the next life'. Reborn is right. (*Folds the newspaper clumsily*). What kind of rubbish is that – in an Irish newspaper. What do we care about that kind of story? (*Pause*). It passes the time, I suppose. (*Pause*). For people who have nothing better to be doing. (*Pause*). Some of us couldn't care less, *a ghrá*, if you came back as an elephant in the next life. (*Slaps the newspaper across his knees*). An ass more like it! (*Leaves the newspaper on the floor beside him. Seems slightly emotional. Places his hands on the arms of the chair as if about to stand up, but doesn't. Sits back in the chair again. Looks towards Danny's room, listens for the sound of running water*). I hope he doesn't drown in the shower whatever he does, he's so long in there. Ah, he will not. He couldn't be drowned, sure you can't drown a fella in a shower. If he was in the bath now, it'd be a different story altogether. Baths are a more dangerous thing. It's much easier drown a fella in a bath. But seeing as there's no bath upstairs, he'll be grand, so he will. (*Pause*). Anyways, isn't he the one who's supposed to be looking after me and not the other way round. (*Laughs*). (*Pause*). It's only that our poor auld Danny likes the shower. A shower in the morning and a shower in the evening. Another one in the middle of the day. You'd think it was over in America he was with all his showers. Sure we had no baths or showers when we were growing up – once or twice a year maybe … and of course we'd go swimming in the summer – and Christ, there was no smell off of us. Or if there was, there was the same smell off of us all so you never got it, cause it was sort of built into our systems, built into our skins, like. (*Knock on the door. COLEMAN sits up in the chair*).

COLEMAN: Who is it?

MAGGIE (*Outside, cheerfully*): It's nobody, Coleman. It's only ghosts and fairies knocking at your door. (*Laughs heartily. MAGGIE enters*).

COLEMAN: The same to you, Maggie, but you're welcome anyhow. Give us an auld kiss, *a ghrá!* (*He turns his cheek to her and MAGGIE dutifully gives him a kiss. She looks around her suspiciously and then looks towards Darach's room*).

MAGGIE: You're alright, Maggie. Darach is gone out, you can relax.

MAGGIE: Oh, thank God for that. How are you anyways, Coleman?

COLEMAN: Ah, up and down, Maggie, *a ghrá*, up and down. But I'm thinking I'm more down than up now these days,

MAGGIE: *Ara*, you are now, Coleman. You're looking great. You're only thinking that.

COLEMAN: And Christ, they're at me these days. The nerves, if you get me? When the auld nerves are at a fella …. I'm thinking, Maggie, I'd be better off dead than the way I am.

MAGGIE (*Blessing herself*): Mother of God, Coleman, but don't be talking like that. You know I don't like talking about the next life when we haven't left this one.

COLEMAN: And I don't like thinking about this life … And anyways I'm talking about death, not about the next life. Sure there hardly is a next life anyways.

MAGGIE: A, give it up, Coleman, *a ghrá*. You're coming to the bingo, aren't you? That'll do you good.

COLEMAN: Flipping right I'm coming out to the bingo, Maggie. Anything to get me out of this place. Sure we might win the jackpot between us. (*Rubbing his palms together*). I was only one number short of it the last night, so I was … all I needed was the legs eleven (*Sticks two fingers in the air. Maggie frowns*). But they give out the numbers too fast, Maggie.

MAGGIE: That reminds me, Coleman (*Taking an envelope out of her coat pocket*). I have some more coupons for you. I nearly forgot them.

COLEMAN: Lyons Tea, is it?

MAGGIE: Lyons Tea, of course. There's eight of them on this card. I said to myself, if I get the big box, I said, there'll be eight tokens on it and you'd be able to put in for the car competition.

COLEMAN: Forty of them you need, isn't it, and I have thirty-two of them already. Some day now when you have time, you must fill in the card for me … cause of the auld shakes in my hand, you know …

MAGGIE: And I have Weetabix tokens for you as well, Coleman, if you're collecting them, but there's no big prizes out of the Weetabix.

COLEMAN: Feck-all except them tin Weetabix boxes, although they have exercise bikes sometimes. (*Thinks*). Didn't we send away a rake of them there a month ago?

MAGGIE: But the Lyons Tea coupons are the most important ones.

COLEMAN: Jesus, Maggie, can you imagine the *craic* we'd have if we won the car. We could go to Bingo in it every Wednesday. (*Pause*). And courting.

MAGGIE What are you saying to me?

COLEMAN: We could go out courting in the car, Maggie, the two of us, like, on the quiet.

MAGGIE (*Agreeing with him for the sake of it*): We could, of course.

COLEMAN: But Maggie, there'd be only one small problem there. None of us can drive. And you can't drive a car without a driver. (*Rather disappointedly raises both hands like a driver's hands on a steering-wheel*).

MAGGIE: We'd have to hire a driver, I suppose.

COLEMAN: We would. (*Disappointed*). That'd make a hames of our courting. He'd be looking back in the mirror at the two of us in the back seat instead of looking at where he was going.

MAGGIE: He'd have us killed on the road, ourselves and the driver, and may two or three others as well.

COLEMAN: You wouldn't mind being dead but we'd be mortified. The small papers would have great headlines out of us.

MAGGIE: Mother of God! We'd be there for the whole world to see.

COLEMAN: In front of the living and the dead! (*Pause*). Do you think that's the reason so many are killed on the roads, Maggie. I read in the paper last week that there was nearly five hundred killed on the roads in Ireland last year ... isn't that an awful lot ... sure half of them might have been courting? (*Pause*). I'm not saying it's the worst way to go ... to die courting I'm saying, not being killed on the road ... but you could be doing worse things when your time comes ... (*Maggie is listening out of politeness, and doesn't bother contradicting him. She obviously doesn't like the topic of conversation, but neither is she too upset by it. She rearranges things and tidies around the house. Prolonged pause*).

COLEMAN: I'm sorry, Maggie. I'm sorry, loveen. I'm talking too much and I forgot that you don't like talking about these things.

MAGGIE: You're alright, Coleman. Sure I've heard it all before.

(*Pause*).

COLEMAN: Oh, Danny's in the shower.

MAGGIE: Hah?

COLEMAN: Danny is up taking a shower, I said.

MAGGIE: Oh!

COLEMAN: He likes his showers. He says they relax him. The muscles.

MAGGIE: Oh, I'd say they do.

COLEMAN: He has three or four showers some days.

MAGGIE: Would you believe that ... I have a sister over in America and she practically lives in the shower. Our Bridie. Any time I ring her, she's inside in the shower. She has a phone in the shower, would you believe. She lives in Florida and sure the heat over there, it'd kill a nigger.

COLEMAN: But sure, that's America for you. Sure we have neither sun nor heat here ... only the rain, the cold and the damp.

MAGGIE: Oh, Mother of God, well, my bones know all about it.

COLEMAN: Washing himself he does be – Danny.

MAGGIE: Hah?

COLEMAN: Danny. I said, he does be washing himself in the shower. But do you think he's up to something when he's in there that often?

MAGGIE: Oh, Mother of God! (*Maggie is disgusted. Covers her mouth*).

COLEMAN (*Teasing*): Ask him now when he comes down, will you? (*The door to Danny's room opens and he appears at the head of the stairs. He's wearing tracksuit bottoms and a light jersey. His hair is washed and he looks well scrubbed*).

DANNY: Howya, Maggie. I didn't hear you come in. (*Comes downstairs. MAGGIE staring at him. She takes a step back*). I must have been in the shower.

MAGGIE: Oh, sure you can hear nothing in the shower. Don't you always see them in the films, breaking into houses and robbing them when they know people are in the shower. (*To Coleman*). I suppose we should be making tracks, so? The bus'll be here any minute. Are you ready?

COLEMAN (*Standing up*): Ready? Sure I've been ready to go since we came back from the last bingo.

DANNY (*To Coleman*): Your coat. (COLEMAN *puts his coat on, slowly and rather awkwardly, with help from Danny.*) Good luck to ye. I hope ye win something.

COLEMAN (*Going out the door*): No matter whether we win or lose. As long as Maggie is not killed here on the road, it doesn't matter.

DANNY: I'd say now you take up more of the road than Maggie. (*Closes the door after them*).

DANNY: Thanks be to Jesus! (*Walks around the kitchen a couple of times, dejectedly*). Bingo, bingo, bingo … (*Shakes his head. Pause. Smirks*). Wednesday. Wednesday. (*Pensively as if a thought had just occurred to him. Sits down and takes up the tabloid newspaper. Flicks through it. Seems to stare at one photograph in particular. He has his two legs spread shamelessly. Scratches his testicles. Stops. Draws his arm across his chest. Looks over his shoulder as if he thinks there is someone behind his back. Folds the paper and leaves it aside. Stands up. He goes over to the window and draws the curtains. Goes to the door and bolts it. A thought strikes him and he unbolts it again. Stands, thinking. Looks around the house. Goes towards the stairs, and then goes upstairs. He glances around the house and towards the door anxiously before entering his room. Closes the door. Once inside the room, he opens a wardrobe. Looks into it. Takes out a full-length dress. Nods his head contentedly and hangs the dress on the back of the door. Turns around and takes off his jersey and his track-suit bottoms, leaving them on the bed. Stands in front of the mirror wearing only his underpants, his back turned to the audience. Settles his hair. Looks at his reflection in the mirror. Rubs his chest, caressing imaginary breasts and shakes his upper body a couple of times. Goes to the dressing table on the far side of the bedroom and opens the bottom drawer. Takes out the plastic bag that he had put there earlier. Takes some lingerie – panties and bra – out of the bag. Holds them to his face and breathes deeply. Look of relief in his face. Goes behind the mirror and emerges again wearing the panties. Stands a while in front of his reflection, admiring himself. About to pick up the bra once more when the doorbell rings. He freezes, caught unawares. Stands motionless for an instant).* Fuck! (*Pause*). Maybe I'm hearing things? (*Pause. Listens. The doorbell rings again).* Fuck, fuck! Fuck you – whoever you are. You'd think they'd mind their own business. (*Pulling on a tracksuit and a jersey).* (*Doorbell rings again).* Fuck this place! Fuck Connemara! (*Coming down the stairs).* Whoever it is, he won't be there for long. CO-MING! (*Opens the door. CYNTHIA steps in).*

CYNTHIA: Hi! Surprise, surprise! (*Hands him a bunch of flowers and kisses him).*

DANNY: Cynthia! It's not a surprise – it's a shock (*Obviously in shock and surprised).* I didn't expect to see *you* this evening.

CYNTHIA: Sure it wouldn't be a surprise if you were expecting me, would it? It's not as if I have to make an appointment to see you, or do I? … I saw Darach on his way down to the pub and seeing as it's bingo night I knew you'd be on your own and I said to myself, there and then like, you know, like you might be lonely … (*Flirtatiously).* Why not … (*Hugs him and they kiss – she rather more enthusiastically than he. She notices his indifference).* Are you not happy to see me, Danny?

DANNY: O, I am, Cynthia, sure I am. (*Seems to be making more of an effort).* It's just that you caught me unawares. (*They let go of each other).* I was downstairs and the doorbell frightened the life out of me. I was about to take a shower and –

CYNTHIA: You were, like hell! (*Sniffs at him slightly suspiciously).* I'd say you're fairly well scrubbed as you are. (*Gives him another kiss).*

DANNY: … after taking a shower – that's what I meant to say.

CYNTHIA: Are you sure that you weren't up to anything else?

DANNY: Cynthia! (*Crosses the room and puts the kettle on – by way of a distraction).* Coffee?

CYNTHIA: I was only asking, OK, and besides, there's nothing wrong with that anyways, when I'm not around. I'd even go so far as saying I'd recommend it from time to time. Rather that than you cheating on me.

DANNY: Cynthia!

CYNTHIA: But not to make a habit of it … They say it's not good to make a habit of it. That you get used to your own way of going about things and …

DANNY: Cynthia … you don't give up, do you!!

CYNTHIA: As long as you don't plan to live your life on your own or join the priests or something. I suppose it'd be all right in that case. Doing it to yourself for the rest of your life. (*She places a hand on his crotch. He starts*).

DANNY: Stop, Cynthia, please!

CYNTHIA: Sorry, Danny. Sorry, loveen. It's just that I'm … (*Pause*). It's just that I'm feeling kind of flighty tonight. Flighty and filthy. What's wrong with you anyways. There's only the two of us here. No better time for a quickie. That's all … You've got to loosen up, Danny, and not to be so uptight.

DANNY: Loosen up?

CYNTHIA: You know what I mean. What's wrong with you tonight? (*Takes a step back*). OK, well, maybe it was a bad idea to come here without warning you. Sorry. Just relax now. Breathe in. That's it. Take a deep breath. (*She takes deep breaths, looking at him affectionately*).

DANNY: You just took me by surprise. That's all.

CYNTHIA: Sorry for dragging you down out of your room, even if you were doing nothing special up there.

DANNY: I like my room, that's all.

CYNTHIA: I like your room too. Come on, quick. You'll be able to relax on the bed. (*Goes to the foot of the stairs. Danny is horrified*).

DANNY: Cynthia! Hold up! Hold on a minute! (*Pause*). I have something for you. Surprise! I'll bring it down. OK? (*Cynthia astonished and rather pleased but stays put, thinking. DANNY goes upstairs, looking over his shoulder to check that she is not following him. Once he is in his room, he moves more quickly. Takes off tracksuit bottoms and panties and pulls on his own underpants and puts tracksuit on again. Stuffs bra and panties into bottom drawer. Grabs the dress and shoves it under the bed. Looks around the room to make sure that everything is in order and looks for something to take with him, anxiously. Takes a small box from the dressing table and is about to go out the door when he realises that he has tucked his jersey into the tracksuit bottoms. Pulls jersey out and comes out of the room, slowly working his way downstairs).*

DANNY: Ah … It's only something small.

CYNTHIA: Flavoured (*Taking the box of condoms*). Strawberry, Passion Fruit … Banana.

DANNY: Well! What do you think?

CYNTHIA: *Very* interesting. They'd be worth a try anyhow. You should try everything once. I'd start with the banana! (*About to feel him up when he takes a few steps back*).

DANNY: Later. Do you want coffee?

CYNTHIA: I suppose I do, for starters! (*Laughs. Takes some condoms out of the box*).

DANNY: For starters! And for desert, there's biscuits or Swiss roll.

CYNTHIA: Swiss roll – without a doubt. What flavour?

DANNY: Chocolate.

CYNTHIA: Chocolate. Nice. Fattening, but nice. They say chocolate gives you extra energy, don't they? Did you know that?

DANNY: Really! (*Teasing*). Too much energy you have, sometimes.

CYNTHIA: Ah? And it cheers people up too. They don't get as depressed. You should eat a piece of chocolate every day. I read that in the *Reader's Digest*.

DANNY: Did you?

CYNTHIA: Darach should eat a bit of chocolate every hour and he mightn't be as cranky as he is.

DANNY: You just have to stay out of his way, as far as you can.

CYNTHIA: As far as you can. (*Pause*). Leave a few slices for him anyhow, though I'd say the whole thing wouldn't be enough for that fella. (DANNY *hands her a cup of coffee and a slice of Swiss roll*).

CYNTHIA: Will we sit down?

DANNY: We will, I suppose. (DANNY *dims the lights slightly. They both sip their coffee. Eat some cake. Look lovingly into each other's eyes. Their free hand around each other. Then they set their cups to one side. Half-stretched on the long chair, entwined and kissing each other for a while, without overdoing it. Cynthia obviously in the mood for more*).

DANNY: Easy, tiger!

CYNTHIA: Did you not bolt the door?

DANNY: I did not bolt the door.

CYNTHIA: *Ara*, I don't mind a bit of danger anyways. (*Ups the ante*). It adds to the excitement.

DANNY: Not here, it doesn't. If the auld fella comes back early from the bingo. Or if they've missed the bus.

CYNTHIA: But sure, your auld fella's blind?

DANNY: But Maggie isn't. That one can see in the dark. She's like an auld cat.

CYNTHIA: Like a cat?

DANNY: Yeah. Cats can find their way in the dark. Like your hands! (*Lights fade gradually*).

CYNTHIA: I'll just feel you up so.

DANNY: Feel away, *a stór*.

CYNTHIA: Ups and downs …

DANNY (*After a while*): Sit over here on my lap so. (*Hug each other lovingly. Long pause. Squeeze each other from time to time. Innocuous music*).

CYNTHIA: Danny! (*Pause*). Will you marry me? (DANNY *sighs*).

DANNY (*Earnestly*): I thought I answered that question before.

CYNTHIA: But I'd like to hear the answer again.

DANNY (*Half-jokingly*): Ask me the question again so.

CYNTHIA: Will you marry me?

DANNY: I'll marry you, Cynthia. You bet. I'll marry you.

CYNTHIA: But when, Danny? (*Rather impatiently*). (DANNY *kisses her*).

DANNY: I don't know (*pause*) yet …

CYNTHIA (*Teasingly, like old gummy woman*): We're not getting any younger you know.

DANNY (*Teasingly in return*): We're not that old either, my dear.

CYNTHIA (*Solemnly*): I know we're not, but that's no way of looking at things. (*They both laugh*). It's time we settled down properly. (*Lights fade further, slowly, but are not dimmed completely. They hold each other tightly. Gentle music. Obviously in the advanced stages of foreplay. They kiss passionately. Lights off. Tick-tock indicates the passing of time. Pause. They lie on each other. Door opens and DARACH enters, well-oiled. Turns on the light. The two sit up straight. They are startled, having been awoken*).

DARACH: Oh-oh! Am I interrupting? (*The two are taken aback and sit up*).

DANNY: You're back.

DARACH: Oh Christ, I am not, Danny. (*Sarcastically*). I am not. (*Takes off his coat and walks round the house*). I'm still down in the pub, with a shower of Man United cunts roaring their heads off. Do ya not see I have a half-pint in my hand and another one sitting in front of me on the counter? (*Walks around. DANNY pulls up his tracksuit bottoms and CYNTHIA fixes her own clothes. They are both slightly embarrassed and try to keep their backs turned to Darach who is standing up and staring at them, at Cynthia in particular and enjoying their predicament*). You're only dreaming I'm back. It's a bad dream in the middle of your … of your … Nightmare.

CYNTHIA: I wish.

DARACH: Ah?

CYNTHIA: Nothing.

DARACH: Nothing is right. And how is Cynthia anyways? (*Gives her an air kiss*). Our Cynthia. Well, nearly … some time … Probably.

CYNTHIA: Alright!

DARACH: Alright! Is that all you are? Only alright and you with your loverboy and getting the …. r (*Pause*) rub. Wouldn't you think you'd be dynamite after that. Or maybe he's no good. (*Pause*). Maybe he's not up to much, the poor creature.

DANNY (*To Cynthia*): Don't bother with him.

DARACH: Don't bother with the beggar's son and he won't bother you. (*To Cynthia*). Sure I can't help it. Coming home after a drink and all I want is to sit down on the couch for a while. And what do I see – but you spread-eagled there in front of me. (*Pause*). One leg pointing out towards the Aran Islands and the other one pointing up to the Connemara mountains. (*Laughs*). D'ya know what's wrong with the pair of ye now … you're not rubbing each other enough … hard enough, like. It's that rubbing makes the sparks and the flames , do ya see.

DANNY: What's it to you?

DARACH: Oh, it makes no odds to me, and I couldn't care less. I'm only giving you good advice for free.

DANNY: We don't want your advice.

DARACH: Well, that's the great thing about advice, ya see. You can take it or leave it. But they say the best things in life are free. Is there a drop of tae in the pot, is there? (*Goes over to the range*).

CYNTHIA: Have a look and you'll know.

DARACH (*Mimicking her*): Have a look and you'll know! Christ but aren't you the touchy one now and you not even in your own house. I'd hate to see you on your own doorstep. Isn't that a fine way to speak to the man of the house. (*Pause*). And when are you two going to give us the day out anyways? You're long enough sniffing at each other at this stage.

DANNY: What's it got to do with you, anyways. (*Tiring of his questioning*).

DARACH: It goes colder as it grows older, isn't that what they say? I'm thinking that's what's wrong with you, you know. But we could have a good day out all the same. The two sides getting together. The Ros Muc gang you see. Handy with the auld knives they are. Jabbing. And if you couple that with the Inis Maan breed, sure you could knock sparks out o' clay. Lethal, darling, lethal. (*Insulting laugh*). (CYNTHIA *looks at Danny as if to seek support*).

DANNY (*To Darach*): You spend your life insulting people. And as for your day out, you'll not be there, so forget it.

DARACH: I won't be there, or it's not going to happen – which is it? (*Pause*). I wouldn't lower myself to going anyways. As if there'd be anyone right at it anyways. I'd have more respect for myself.

DANNY: And no respect for anyone else.

DARACH (*To Cynthia*): It's just that I'd like to be able to give my little brother away, ya see, Cynthia. To get rid of him. To see the back of him for the last time. *Ara*, sure you could hardly expect the auld fella – him with his blackthorn stick and his gammy walk – to be crawling up the aisle on those bandy sticks he has for legs. Sure he'd only trip himself up – as well as anyone else who was unfortunate enough to be around him.

CYNTHIA: Only women are given away, Darach. Not men. Do you know anything at all about weddings?

DARACH (*Insulted*): Look it now, Miss Mickileen Marcas an Doireen, you can be making your way home, so you can. You're in my house now and don't you forget it.

CYNTHIA: Now, look who's touchy!

DARACH: You're not here looking after the auld fella. (CYNTHIA *puts on her coat*).

DANNY: Look it –

DARACH: Look it now yourself –

CYNHIA: And God forbid I'd ever have to spend time in your company. (DANNY *shows her out*).

DARACH: I could stop you from darkening my door … a Barring Order.

CYNTHIA: You could not, you know, because then you wouldn't be able to be picking on me. And that's what keeps you going, picking on people. You couldn't live without that. (CYNTHIA *and* DANNY *leave, closing the door after them. Danny has no coat on, and is obviously just seeing her to the door.* DARACH *laughs – sneering victorious laugh*).

DARACH: Feck the pair of ye. (*Walks around the room, with a mug of tea in his hand. Spots a bunch of flowers on the table. Picks it up and smells them*). Flowers. (*Pause. Sarcastically*). Ah, ain't that sweet! (*Looks disparagingly at the flowers. Then rubs them in a circular motion against his crotch and grimaces. He extends his rear and strokes the flowers against his bottom, as though using them to wipe it, mouthing the sound of flatulence at the same time. He then spits at them. He frowns and looks around as if looking for a hiding place for the flowers, or is about to do something mischievous with them when* DANNY *walks in. Throws the flowers to* DANNY *who catches them, though he has been caught unawares*).

DARACH: Your flowers, Danny. I was having a look at them. There's a fine smell off of them. I'd say they set her back a few Yo-Yos, so they did. (*Scowls at Danny*).

DANNY: They're no concern of yours. Leaving your big ugly paw marks on them. (*Leaves them on the table as though contaminated*).

DARACH: For all I know they could had been for myself or for the auld fella – I don't see your name written on them or nothing, like. I'm thinking she has a soft spot for me, ya see. (*Pause*). She might know that I have something you don't.

DANNY: You're as thick as my hole.

DARACH: And is your hole thick? Well now, that's news to me – not that I'm any the wiser now that I know, mind you … And I should have known … I should have asked Cynthia. (DANNY *goes up to his room hurriedly*).

DANNY: You know nothing. That's your problem. And you don't want anyone else to have anything.

DARACH: Ah, blather.

DANNY: Fuck you, ya cunt!

DARACH: Well fuck you too, twice over! (DANNY *storms up to his room and bangs the door after him. Lies down on the bed then sits up and stares, fuming. DARACH shrugs his shoulder, not having expected a tongue-lashing. Takes the flowers and puts them back. Stares blankly*). (*In the next part of the scene, the two rant about each other, in their respective rooms. Each is clearly annoyed with the other. Some gaps in the speech, but at other times they both speak at the same time. This doesn't matter – the stage separates them anyway. Each paces his own ground. The audience swings its attentions to them in turn. Anger building up inside each of them until it reaches a climax*).

DANNY: Cunt!

DARACH: Stupid cunt!

DANNY: I can't stick that bastard any longer.

DARACH: Pig (*getting up*).

DANNY: He only wants to be annoying other people (*getting up*).

DARACH: I wouldn't mind but herself. That one'll walk all over him yet, and it'll be good enough for him. She'll leave him there.

DANNY: Stupid bastard!

DARACH: If she only knew what he is like. Ah, Jesus, she was on fire tonight.

DANNY: And talking like that to Cynthia.

DARACH: But I got her nicely with the smellers. Ha-Ha-Ha! That'll sort her out. Turncoat!

DANNY: You can't win with him. Even if you don't open your mouth he tries to get one up on you.

DARACH: She hadn't much to say for herself going out the door, the slut! Silent, *a mhac*. Silent as a dummy.

DANNY: And how could my fucking life be normal.

DARACH: If it weren't for the auld fella, I'd knock the shite out of him. But as soon as he kicks the bucket ...

DANNY: If it weren't for the auld fella, I wouldn't be here.

DARACH: And it mightn't be long more now ...

DANNY: Sneaking around in other people's lives.

DARACH: Up there in that room. (*Looking up sideways*).

DANNY: You can't do nothing in this house.

DARACH: Locking the door on his way in and locking it again on his way out. (*Short pause. The two are thinking*).

DANNY: But it won't be long now.

DARACH: Wait till I go up to him.

DANNY: 'Fuck's sake! It's about time he was put in his place.

DARACH: What he needs now is a good root, the cunt! A good root!

DANNY (*Clenched fist and boiling with rage*): Cunt! (*At this point Danny is at the back of the room looking behind him and Darach is at the front of the kitchen looking out in front of him, so that they are more or less above and below each other.*) Cunt! (*Heads towards the door. At the same time Darach is at the foot of the stairs. DANNY comes out of his room*).

DARACH: Look at what's coming down the stairs. And where are you going, I wonder?

DANNY: You won't be wondering for much longer! (*Both look ready for a fight*). (*Pause for a second, each seeming surprised that the other is prepared to take him on*).

COLEMAN (*Outside, sings*): 'Humpty Dumpty sat on a wall. Humpty Dumpty had a great fall ...' (*Danny and Darach stand petrified. The front door opens and COLEMAN comes in, all excited. MAGGIE is with him, helping him in*). (*to Danny*). Tinky. (*to Darach*). Winky! (*Lifting a Tellytubby triumphantly*). Look. I won another Tellytubby in the raffle tonight. Tinky Winky. That's three of them I have now. Laa-Laa is the only one I'm missing.

MAGGIE: Mind yourself on that mat, Coleman. Mind you don't break your neck.

COLEMAN: Thanks, Maggie.

DARACH (*Turning away*): Some chance of him falling, some chance. *Ara*, fuck it! (*Danny has come down the stairs at this stage*).

DANNY: Come in, Maggie. (*Darach moves though the house, as though getting out of the way, isolating himself somewhat*).

MAGGIE: I'll come in for two minutes.

DARACH: Two minutes, my eye!

COLEMAN (*To Danny*): But they robbed me of the jackpot.

DANNY: Did they now? Sit down there, Maggie, and have a mug of tea.

DARACH: Ah Christ, the same auld story – and it's mouldy at this stage.

COLEMAN: They really did rob me this time.

DANNY: Did they?

COLEMAN: I shouted 'bingo' but they never told me I had filled the wrong page. Sure they didn't, Maggie?

MAGGIE: It was a mix-up, Coleman, a little mix-up.

DARACH: And it wasn't just the pages were mixed up.

MAGGIE (*To Coleman*): You didn't notice them going on to the next page. (*To Danny*). And he stayed on the page he was on.

DARACH (*Looking at Coleman*): Stupid gom!

MAGGIE: It was only a small mistake that couldn't be helped.

DARACH: Sure mistakes wouldn't be mistakes if they could be helped.

MAGGIE (*Wounded*): Now, now.

DARACH: If you had kept an eye on him, it wouldn't have happened to him.

DANNY: Sure it's none of your business anyways. Nobody asked you anything. (*Pause*).

DARACH: And isn't it well for me. Pity I'm not deaf as well.

COLEMAN: But what odds? We had great *craic* on the bus, Danny. Didn't we, Maggie?

MAGGIE: O indeed and we did.

DANNY: Wonderful.

COLEMAN: A lovely sing-song.

DANNY: Ye were singing.

COLEMAN: Cripes, we were. (*Singing*). 'The Rocky Road to Dublin. One, two, three, four, five'.

DARACH: Like an auld rusty saw on dry timber I suppose.

MAGGIE (*Who has decided to take her leave*): I'll see you tomorrow or the day after, please God.

DANNY: Drop of tea?

MAGGIE: Ah, I won't have any tea, thanks Danny, loveen. It's getting late. Another time.

DANNY: But the kettle'll be boiled in two minutes.

DARACH: Didn't you hear her saying she didn't want no tea? She might be in a hurry home to recite the Rosary for the walls to hear.

COLEMAN: Leave poor auld Maggie alone, now, the creature, and the way she looks after me every Wednesday.

DARACH: The cat purrs to please itself.

MAGGIE (*At the door*): Goodnight now, loveens.

COLEMAN: Goodnight now, and thanks again, Maggie.

DARACH: Before you go, Maggie, just one little thing to say I'm sorry if I was rotten to you earlier on … There's a bunch of flowers on the table there. Well, they're not mine; they're Danny's (*pause*) but this isn't really a flowers sort of a house, being full of nettles and all … He might want to give them to you to put in the church in the morning. (*Maggie shocked. Danny surprised. They look at each other*).

DANNY: If you'd like them, Maggie, take them with you, by all means, for the church.

MAGGIE: I'll take them with me so, and thanks very much. (*Picking them up*). Well now, they're gorgeous. (*Sniffs them*).

And they smell lovely. Their grand and fresh. Are you sure you don't want them yourself?

DANNY: You're grand. Put them in the church.

MAGGIE: I will not – I'll put them in the grotto on my way home. Our Lady's Grotto.

DARACH: Our Lady's Grotto. (*Grins broadly, though no-one else understands why. MAGGIE goes home. Uneasy, prolonged pause. DARACH and DANNY glance at each other uneasily*).

COLEMAN (to DANNY): Will you undo my laces like a good man, and I'll be away to bed. The bed has to be made too.

DANNY: OK. OK. Will you not have a cup of tea first?

COLEMAN: *Ara* no, I won't. I had any amount of tea and buns at the bingo. I don't want to be running to the loo all night. (*DANNY bends down and unties Coleman's shoelaces and helps him take off his shoes. He then goes back into Coleman's room. COLEMAN follows him*).

DARACH (*Looking behind him, grinning sarcastically*): Why don't you sing him a lullaby; something that might send him to sleep and stop him ranting and raving and keeping me awake. (*Danny and Coleman are in the other room by now. Pause. He looks around the stage, as if to suggest he doesn't know what to do now that he's on his own. He seems rather disappointed that there is no-one left to pick on. Looks forlorn. Thinks. Pause. Bolts the front door and winds the clock. Goes into his own room dejectedly and bolts the door after him. Pause. DANNY returns from Coleman's room. Looks around, somewhat surprised that Darach is no longer there. Looks at his [Darach's] bedroom door. Goes to the front door and is about to bolt it when he realises that it has already been bolted. Goes over to the dresser and takes down the clock which he is about to wind until he discovers it has already been wound. Looks at Darach's bedroom door again. Stands silently a while. Then he smiles. Goes upstairs. Turns off the kitchen light and turns on the light in his own room. Sits down and breathes a sigh of relief*).

DANNY: Thanks be to Christ. (*Pause*). Thank God for nights. (*Pause. He appears to be listening to the sound of silence. Stand up and opens the wardrobe door. Takes off his clothes, down to his underpants. Takes some lingerie – bra and panties – out of the wardrobe. Holds them up to the light, affectionate. Seems happier now, and more at ease with himself. Pause. Stands behind the mirror, humming to himself. When he returns he is wearing the panties).*

(*In a high-pitched voice*): Close your eyes, now, Danny. Close your eyes. (*Stands in front of the mirror, settling himself exactly in the middle. Back to audience*). Da-na! (*Prances around and looks at himself in the mirror, extending his arms like a dancer. Wiggles his rear*). You look gor-geous, Danny. You'd think they were made to measure. (*Takes down the bra*). And now, for the padding. Padding is a very precise business. (*Takes two socks out of the drawer and stuffs them into the cups. Puts on the bra, standing in front of the mirror. Looks at himself awhile. Takes some long dresses out of the wardrobe, measuring them against himself before he decides which one to wear. Puts it on. Then takes a long wig out of the top of the wardrobe and puts it on. Brushes his hair. Takes a make-up bag and carefully applies some lipstick. Looks at his reflection once more. Takes a pair of tights and a pair of high-heels from the bottom of the wardrobe. Rummages around until he finds a matching bag. Struts around the room, smiling and obviously very pleased with himself, with exaggerated feminine gestures. Pretends he's on the telephone.*

(*Falsetto voice 1*): Are you going to the social this evening?

(*Falsetto voice 2*): Oh, not tonight, Josephine. I've nothing to wear.

(*Falsetto voice 1*): What are you doing tomorrow? I'm free tomorrow. O, smashing! Me too. We could go shopping. Kookaï have some gorgeous things in the window. The very latest.

(*Falsetto voice 2*): I'll give you a tinkle in the morning so. Sound, Josephine, Sound as a bell. (*Puts on a CD, low volume. Gentle classical music. Sits at ease, knees together in a very feminine fashion. Long pause while he relaxes. 'Poses' unknown to himself. Then stops in his tracks as if a thought has just occurred to him. Pause. His face gradually grows sad. Places a hand on his breast.*

Lights dim slightly). I was seven years of age, well almost eight I suppose, because it happened in March, and it was very cold. Very cold. I can't remember now what the play was but we were rehearsing for the Patrick's day show. There were two plays put on that day – one by the boys' school and the other from the girls'. (*Pause*). And we were all messing on the stage until the teacher lined us up and started giving out the parts. (*Pause*). There's one girl's part in the play, she said, looking over and back. Twice she looked over and back and then she looked at me. (*Pause*). Danny, she said, you can be the girl. You have a lovely soft voice. I didn't mind at first, but then the older boys started sniggering. And then I got embarrassed and didn't want to do the part at all. (*Pause*). But she made me. (*Pause*). A week later we had the dress rehearsal. She opened out a big bag of clothes and dressed everyone. I have dresses for you, she says. You can leave your trousers on for rehearsals, but not for the real performance, she says. You're a poor sad little girl, but all that is going to change because you're going to marry the rich prince, then you'll be a princess. You'll be wearing an old raggedy dress in the first scene, but then in the second scene you'll have a lovely silky dress with golden lace on it. All the parents will be clapping with delight. (*Pause*). And the night we had the final rehearsal three of the other boys dared me. They dared me to wear girls' knickers under the dress. They dared me a pound each. Three pounds altogether. Big money. They had found a pair of knickers in the bag of clothes. I didn't mind risking it but (*pause*) when I put them on and put the dress on over them, they felt (*pause*), they felt so comfortable, so smooth, the fine silk slipping over my skin, as light and as easy as a butterfly … and in a peculiar way I felt that my body was free … so free. (*Pause*). Not tight and tied up like it feels when I'm wearing trousers. I felt I could nearly fly, I was so free in my new clothes. No. I felt I'd been given a new body. No. I felt I'd discovered my own body. (*Pause*). Discovered something for the first time, something I'd never missed until I found it. (*Pause*). And I wore them every night after that without saying a word to anyone, and I didn't want the weekend to come and then on the last night, when I saw all the clothes being thrown on the ground and the teacher stuffing them into black plastic bags … (*Pause*). I felt sorry for the clothes. (*Pause*). Next day I went to the priest with the three pounds and asked him to say Mass for my mother. 'Of course, my child', he said. 'Of course, although I know your Mammy is in heaven already, I'll say another Mass for her and I'll pray for you too and for all the family. But here, son, keep this money yourself. Buy yourself a few sweets or maybe you'd like to buy new football shorts or a new Galway jersey', (*emotional*) and he shoves the money down into my pocket. (*Pause*). He did. (*Pause*). Shoves it in. (*Telephone rings downstairs. Lights up to bring him back to reality*). Fuck! (*Startled. Jumps up. Stands petrified as if he can't believe his ears until the phone starts ringing*). Fuck! Fuck! Fuck you! What if it's for me? (*Pulls off his shoes and socks, his wig and stuffs them under the bed, while trying to take of the dress with the free hand*). They're going to wake up. (*Wearing only a bra and panties, wraps a towel around his waist. About to go downstairs when he realises he is still wearing a bra. Fumbles with the clasp but cannot undo it. Grabs another towel, wraps it around his back and holds it up in front. Turns on the light at the head of the stairs. Runs downstairs. At the same time,* DARACH *emerges from his own room, wearing drawers and a T-shirt, but* DANNY *gets to the phone before him. Danny is nervous as Darach is standing by his side listening*). Hello. Hello. Yes, Cynthia! (*Letting Darach know that the call is not for him and that he should clear off*). I was in bed. (*Lips turned in as he is still wearing lipstick*). (DARACH *sulks and notices that Danny is acting very peculiarly. He stares at him as though perplexed, particularly by the way Danny has the towel over his shoulders and is holding it in one hand*). Oh, really. And when. (*Pause*). I know, Cynthia. I did. (*Pause*). I'm OK. I'm OK. I'll be able to do it in the morning so. Don't worry. Ah? (*Pause*). Cynthia! (*Audible tension in his voice*). I don't want to talk about it now. Tomorrow. Ah? (*Darach still doesn't look like he's leaving. Thinks for a while and then goes over to the sink and fills a glass of water. Drinks it slowly. Then washes his hands.*

Looks around him, as if looking for a towel to dry his hands and walks towards Danny whose back is turned to him, listening to Cynthia. Listens carefully as though he feels they are talking about him. Starts drying his hands with the towel on Danny's shoulder). OK. OK. *(Impatiently).* Good night Cynthia. We'll talk about it tomorrow. Sure. *(Speech accelerates)* Night –

DARACH: Is that my towel you have, anyways, is it?

DANNY: It is not – *(But at this stage DARACH has swiped the towel from his shoulders, meeting some resistance. They are both in shock and there is a brief poignant moment of silence. DANNY looks down, his hand still on the telephone. DARACH stares at Danny's body. Bursts out laughing, mockingly).*

DARACH: Christ all fucking Mighty! Jesus, Mary and fucking saint Joseph. What have we got here then? The Rose of Tralee. *(Pause).* Miss Universe herself! *(Pause).* Peigín Letter fucking More! *(Danny stands mortified).*

DANNY: Would you ever fuck off. Just fuck off! *(Seething with anger).*

DARACH *(Laughing like a drain)*: Fuck off is it? Can the cat not look at the Queen? *(Drops the towel as though it were contaminated and frowns. Dries his hands on his T-shirt staring all the while at Danny. Reverses into his own room as if Danny was carrying some infectious disease).* Jesus! *(Pause).* Aren't you some fucking sight for sore eyes. *(Blackout).*

Interval

Act Two

Scene One

In the sitting room/kitchen, the following morning. DARACH *is walking around with a slice of toast in one hand and a mug of tea in the other. Humming. Seems to be in no hurry. Sings, looking up towards Danny's room:*

> 'Is ó goirim, goirim í, goirim í mo stór;
> We'll all go to Peggy's house, cause Peggy is a whore'.

COLEMAN *enters slowly from the bedroom, half-dressed.*

DARACH (*To himself*): The dead arose. (*In good form. To Coleman*). You didn't die in your sleep anyways.

COLEMAN: O, I did you know, but I've arisen from the dead. Bit like a cat. You'll have to put up with me for another day.

DARACH: We will, I suppose, or for a bit of a day anyhow. Don't count your chickens before they hatch , like – it's many a man was fighting fit in the morning, you know, and was dead as a doornail – D.E.A.D. – that same evening, or by lunchtime even, isn't it true for me?

COLEMAN: It is, I suppose, seeing as you say it yourself. (*Pause. Watches him eat*). A fella could die of hunger too, you know.

DARACH: He could, but not in this country he couldn't. I suppose he could maybe in Africa, or in one of those countries where you have the black babies with the flies on them. Maybe if the woman of the house got up (*Looks towards Danny's room and raises his voice*) she might throw you out some sort of a breakfast. (*Shouts*). Danny! (*Pause*). Waitress, you're wanted down here! Table number one. Mr Coleman for breakfast! (*Singing to himself: 'And I said what about, breakfast at Tiffany's'*). He mightn't have slept too well last night, you see. That might be why he's late getting up. I didn't sleep a wink. What about yourself?

COLEMAN: I slept grand, indeed. Like a log.

DARACH: I kept waking up. Having nightmares, or bad dreams, like. I kept seeing women with these huge skirts on them flying around the house like big bats. Walking on the ceiling and sticking to it, they were.

COLEMAN: And so what if you did. Women? Sure that was no nightmare. And there's bats there anyway.

DARACH: But they weren't proper women, like. There was something funny about them. You'd swear there was something wrong with them. (*Upstairs*). If you don't get up soon, this fella will have died of starvation. He might be dead in his bed; he might have died last night of breast cancer. Don't they say Connemara is full of cancer, that it's in the rocks. (*To Coleman*). What do you eat in the morning anyways? Weetabix, isn't it?

COLEMAN: Weetabix: Weetabix for breakfast and Weetabix for tea.

DARACH (*Taking them out of the box*): One or two?

COLEMAN: One, unless I'm really hungry, and two when I am.

DARACH: And if you don't mind me asking, how hungry are you this morning?

COLEMAN (*Pause*): In-between, I suppose.

DARACH: In-between, says he. Well does that mean one Weetabix or two?

COLEMAN: One (*pause*) and a half.

DARACH: One and a half! (*Snaps a biscuit in two impatiently*). I wonder now if you'll be needing the big half or the small half this morning, to fill your empty belly.

COLEMAN: The big half. (DARACH *looks at the two halves and out of spite, puts the smaller half into the bowl*).

DARACH: You don't need any sugar in case you'd get diabetes or cholesterol or blood pressure on top of all that ails you already. (*Shoves the bowl into his lap. Sits down and finishes his own mug of tea*).

COLEMAN (*Coyly*): Danny usually puts a little dropeen of milk on them.

DARACH: Does he now. From his tits, is it? Now that's a fucking miracle. (*Going towards the fridge*). Wait till I tell Maggie about these miracles. She'll say that there's power in that grotto. (*Blesses himself sarcastically*). There's slimline here and real milk. (*Takes out two cartons*). We'd better leave the slimline for your wan upstairs. (*Raising his voice*). She's watching the figure, like. Women are hoors like that. They can't eat a bite on Sunday without worrying about the inches that'll appear on the waistline on Monday. (*Pours the milk into Coleman's bowl, but some of the milk spills on the floor as Coleman has a shake in his hand*).

DARACH: A, *muise*, you clumsy auld eejit.

COLEMAN: Sure I can't help it if I have the shakes in that hand.

DARACH: *Ara*, sure you're one big shake. (*Mopping up the spilt milk*). Spill it again, ya *pleib*, and I'll make you go down on your two knees and lick it up like a cat!

COLEMAN: Miaow!

DARACH: Miaow, my hole. Do you want a knife or a fork?

COLEMAN: Neither. I want Chinese Chopsticks. (DARACH *gives him a spoon.* COLEMAN *starts eating greedily.* DANNY *comes downstairs in a dressing gown and slippers. Looks tired and weary*).

DARACH: Ah, will you look – Dolly Parton is getting up. (*Laughs*). Give us your autograph. (*Pause*). We thought you had a woman up there with you, you were so long getting up, for a change. Didn't we Coleman? (DANNY *ignores him. He is obviously annoyed, but keeps a lid on his anger. Checks that there is tea in the pot and water in the kettle and switches it on.* DARACH *takes a few steps back from him and scowls*).

DANNY (*To Coleman who is eating*): Did you have your tea?

COLEMAN: No, not yet.

DARACH: Isn't that your job, making tea for him? If you think I'm going skivvying, you've another think coming. I've a day's work to do. (*Ready to go out the door*). It'd be more in your line than … than … than …

DANNY (*To Darach, suddenly tenacious*): Than what?

DARACH: Than other things. Making an ass of yourself. (*Pause*). You've a face on you that'd stop a clock.

DANNY: You just keep your big gob shut!

DARACH: I'll keep my gob shut … (*Pause. Walks over towards Danny*). Till I feel like opening it. (*Looks at him icily, opens his mouth which emits no sound. Closes his mouth again. Exits*).

COLEMAN: What's wrong with him today, do you know?

DANNY: Good question. (*Takes the bowl from him*). Will you have a mug of tea?

COLEMAN: I didn't enjoy my Weetabix at all today … (*To himself*). I'd much prefer muesli, anyways, but I can't chew it any more. (*Pause*). It's the nuts and the raisins. But Weetabix are easy to swallow. You could take your teeth out to eat them. (DANNY *hands him a mug of tea, having put two spoons of sugar into it. Pause*).

DANNY: Are you all right?

COLEMAN: Was there thunder last night, or is it just me?

DANNY: I don't think there was thunder, though we were promised it alright.

COLEMAN: I thought I heard a few claps, but sure I suppose I must have dreamt it. (*Sips some tea*).

DANNY: There's no harm in dreaming. Is that tea alright?

COLEMAN: It is … as long as a fella's not having nightmares. (*Pause*). Do you know what day it is today, Danny?

DANNY: I do, Dad. The fifteenth. (*Pause*).

COLEMAN: The fifteenth.

DANNY: Mam would be proud of you, Dad, so she would. (*Drinking tea*).

COLEMAN: She'd be proud of you too. Of the way you look after me.

DANNY: Finish your tea, now, and I'll bring you out in a while.

COLEMAN: You'll bring me up to the grave, like a good man.

DANNY: I will.

COLEMAN: And we'll put some fresh flowers on it.

DANNY: We will.

COLEMAN (*To himself, pensively*): Twenty-five years this year. Twenty-five years.

DANNY: I know. Twenty-five years, a special year. A kind of celebration in a way.

COLEMAN: Twenty-five years' worth of flowers ... and of prayers. Twenty-five years' worth of Masses. And they go on and on. (*He goes over to the wall and takes a closer look at an old black and white wedding photograph*).

DANNY: That's the way it is, Dad. Drink up your tea now, like a good man, and don't be tormenting yourself.

COLEMAN: But the years go on and on. Isn't it strange, Danny. In a hundred years' time, she'll be a hundred and twenty-five years dead ... You only live for so many years and you can be dead for ever.

DANNY: You can ... I suppose.

COLEMAN: In a hundred years' time she'll be a hundred and twenty-five years old (*brief pause*) dead. (*Pause*). If you get me. She will, you know.

DANNY: Your tea'll be gone cold, Dad, if you don't drink it up. And you don't like cold tea.

COLEMAN: Indeed, and I do not like cold tea. (*Drinks some. Pause*). Cold tea always reminds me of rain. But this is a grand cup of tea, Danny. Nice and sweet.

DANNY: You'll be alright there while I take a quick shower.

COLEMAN: I will, *a mhac*, I will.

DANNY: You can be drinking your tea.

COLEMAN: I can. You have a nice shower and I'll have a nice cup of tea. (DANNY *goes up to his room and turns on the shower. COLEMAN slowly sips his tea. DANNY can be seen getting into the shower and the sound of water can be heard. Sudden outburst of thunder and lightening. COLEMAN gets a fright, drops the mug and sits up suddenly, frightened*). Oh!

(*Pause*). Jesus Christ! (*Lights flicker once or twice, but the power isn't cut. Torrential rain can be heard and* COLEMAN *looks around as if he had nowhere to take refuge. He is shaking. Sits up in the chair. Pause*). It was early autumn. Dull weather. We were promised rain, so we were, and thunder, only we didn't know it ... (*Pause. Lights cross-fade from Danny's room to Coleman. Rest of scene rather surreal, shower and rain can be heard intermittently in the background. Thunder and lightening*). We'll go out on the bog, says I, and stack that last clamp of turf and that'll be us finished with the bog for this year. Will you come out with me, will you? (*Pause*). She was taking a loaf of bread out of the oven and she didn't speak for a minute in case she burnt herself. I was thinking of doing the washing, she said. We'll be home by tea-time if the two of us go, say I. (*Pause*). Whatever you think yourself, said she. There was no more talk about it. (*Pause*). But Kate liked the bog. She liked the bog air. (*Pause*). We were hardly an hour out there when the skies opened. The lightening struck. We'll leave it to hell, says she. Look at the sky. That rain is torrential ... For the sake of five minutes, says I. Sure if we get wet itself, what harm. We won't melt. (*Pause*). We'll have the bog over with for this year ... and we kept going like the clappers ... the sky alive with lightening. But we took no notice of it. (*Pause*). Then a flash struck me and I was all dizzy. I fell ... My head was splitting when I tried to get up and wasn't I struck a second time. I was. But if I was, it didn't knock me this time ... but when I looked over to where Kate was, I couldn't see her at all. It might be because I'm dizzy, I said to myself in the beginning ... but when I looked over, didn't I see her on the flat of her back in the heather. (*Pause*). I went over to help her up ... not thinking for a minute that she wouldn't get up like I did myself ... and I having been hit twice ... she had her eyes open, like there was a light in them ... but she made no attempt to raise her hand, so that I'd help her up off the ground ... there wasn't a twitch out of her ... and it was then I knew. It was then I knew. (*Lights suddenly go to black*).

Danny's room. Spotlight suddenly focuses on Danny. Sits on the bed staring in front of him. He has just showered. His hair is freshly-combed and he has a towel around his shoulders. He has one of his mother's dresses across his knees. Starts speaking as soon as the light falls on him, so that the story is continued from the previous scene.

DANNY: And when they brought her in they sat her in the chair, and her hair was dripping wet. That's what I remember most – her hair, and she was so particular about it – it was soaking wet now and tangled. Dad and Seáinín Joeen were after carrying her in, and the dress. (*Pause. Pulls apart the pleats of the dress with his two hands*). I got a towel in the hot press and I was going to give it to her to dry her hair, when Maggie took it from me and told me to go to my room, but I didn't. 'Your Mammy isn't well', said Seáinín Joeen when no-one else was talking to me, 'your Mammy is sick'. And they brought her back into the bedroom and lay her down on the bed. We'll look after her if she's sick, said I, until she's better again. She minded me last week when I was sick … But they wouldn't let us into the bedroom, saying that they had to change her clothes, that they were all soaked from being out in the rain. (*Loosens his grip of the dress*). Later on Auntie Baby told us that God had taken Mammy with him and that he had made a lovely place for her in heaven and that she'd be looking down at us and that she'd always be proud of us … and you couldn't keep Darach out of the room after that. He started kicking the door for all he was worth until they let him in … 'Darach'll be alright in a day or two', says Auntie Baby to me, with her arms around me, 'and he'll mind you for your Mam'. And then she burst out crying. (*Pause*). That was the first time I saw a adult crying. (*Pause*). An adult crying. And the night after they buried her I couldn't stop crying; thinking about her down there in the cold, wet clay and me in my nice warm bed … The tears were choking me when Darach elbowed me in the ribs and winded me. 'Shut your mouth', he said, real mad. 'Why don't you stop crying. You weren't Mammy's pet anyways. I was', he said. 'You're Dad's pet ...' And I couldn't cry after that. I couldn't cry. (*Lights suddenly go to black*).

Sitting room/kitchen that same evening. Coleman at the front door, on his way in. Has a handful of leaflets and magazines and he's scanning them as he heads for his chair.

COLEMAN: 'Shall the World Survive?' (*Looking at another one*). 'A Life of Tranquillity in a New World'. (COLEMAN *opens it and holds it up to his eyes, trying to read it. Opens another brochure*). 'What is the Purpose of Life? How Can You Find It?' Hold on till I get my magnifying glass. That print is fierce small. (*Rummaging around until he finds it in his pocket. Sings*). 'She sees the world through rose-coloured glasses, Painted skies and graceful romances'. (*Starts reading slowly*). 'In time, God will reign again on earth and peace will reign; relations among animals and between animals and men will be as they were in the Garden of Eden'. Huh? I wonder what kind of relations they're talking about between animals and men? Ah Christ, I think I'd prefer to be reading the *Sunday World*, but sure they might come in handy some day when I'll have no paper to read. If the papers go on strike. (DARACH *enters. Seems to be in bad form. Sees Coleman flicking though the leaflets*).

DARACH: Was Patrick Jehovah around, was he; with his leaflets?

COLEMAN (*Reads from the leaflets by way of response, looking at Darach*): 'What is the Purpose of Life? How Can You Find it?' He was yeah; Patrick Jehovah was around alright. He must know I like reading. This booklet has all the answers.

DARACH: Oh it has. It has of course (*Takes one of the leaflets out of Coleman's hands*).

COLEMAN: Except that it's a bit late now for the likes of me and my life nearly over. How well he wasn't around fifty years ago. If I had all these answers starting out in life, things might have been better.

DARACH: Blather, auld man. Pig's blather with a hole in it! You'd make some Jehovah. Going around there from morning till night handing out leaflets that nobody wants.

Bloody Jehovah! 'Shall the World Survive?' (*Sarcastically*). He'll be lucky if he survives himself, the yellow-bellied bastard, if he darkens that door again while I'm around … filling old people's heads with that kind of bullshit (*Waves leaflets in the air*). Doesn't he know right well that your brain is scrambled anyways, and that your head is mixed up enough as it is. (*Throws the leaflets on the ground*). (DANNY *enters, holding a carrier bag*).

DANNY: What's going on?

DARACH (*To Danny*): I'll tell you what's going on. Patrick gobshite Jehovah was around spouting bullshit.

DANNY: And what harm if he was? Isn't it a free country? (*Taking messages out of the carrier bag and putting them away. Including two boxes of Weetabix and a box of Lyons Tea*).

DARACH: Every harm.

DANNY: Pay no heed to them if you don't like what they have to say.

DARACH: Exactly, pay no heed to them and hunt them, that's what I'd have done if I was here.

COLEMAN: That Patrick is a nice friendly fella.

DARACH (*To Coleman*): Sneaky and friendly. Isn't that the way they work? (*To Danny*). Isn't his head addled enough as it is without him packing more nonsense into it?

DANNY: Sure if his head is that addled, what difference does it make?

COLEMAN: *Ara*, will ye leave poor Patrickeen alone. Sure he's only doing what he thinks is right – like we all do.

DARACH: Except that he's not just anybody where religion is concerned. Like, did you think he'd have horns on, ya clown?

COLEMAN: Horns? (*Standing up*).

DARACH: Invisible horns. He has them alright. They're the ones you have to watch. You don't see them until they puck you in the back. Those fine Jehovahs. (*To Coleman, half in jest*).

They're the ones now would put a halt to your gambling and your betting. I bet you he didn't tell you that.

COLEMAN: Gambling?

DARACH: Yeah. They're dead set against gambling. And bingo. Bingo's a mortal sin. I wouldn't mind but if you were run-down or ever in need of a drop of blood, they wouldn't give it to you. Not a single drop, even if Galway Bay turned to blood, they'd leave you there till the last drop of your own blood ran dry or till life had sucked if out of you.

COLEMAN: Is that right?

DARACH: That is right. Bloody Jehovahs.

DANNY (*Impatiently*): Would you ever give over?

DARACH: I suppose I could, but I won't.

DANNY (*Giving up*): Sure keep going so.

DARACH: I'll keep going so.

COLEMAN: Keep going then between yourselves, the pair of ye. But I think I'll lie on the bed for a whileen … I only want a bit of peace and quiet, and I'll be able to read these at my leisure. (*Goes back into the room*). (*Pause. Tension*).

DANNY: Look it here. You have the auld fella all confused again.

DARACH: Again! How can you further confuse a fella who has been bamboozled for the last twenty-five years? Ha?

DANNY: Today is Mam's anniversary, I'll have you know.

DARACH: I'll have you know, says he. (*Angry*). Do you think that never occurred to me – or am I a complete *bobarún*? Sure it's well I remember the day she was killed – better than you remember it! And there's a reason for that. Sure you were still in nappies.

DANNY: All I'm saying is that you could be a bit more civilised.

DARACH: Civilised … Well, I supposed I should be more civilised to women alright. I'm really sorry. (*Sarcastically*). Look it now, going on what I saw in this house last night, you have your own problems.

DANNY: I have no problems.

DARACH: Oh, you don't, now, do you not, and I suppose every man in Connemara goes round in his skirt and fucking knickers, does he? (*Sarcastic laugh*) … and what do you think Cynthia'll have to say about these capers. I bet it wasn't she brought you those rags that you squeeze your balls into.

DANNY: Leave Cynthia out of it.

DARACH: I often said that she was the one wearing the trousers, not you (*mocking laugh*) but at least you're wearing the bras. Or you were. Yourself and your boutiqueful of rags and rubbers. Sure you're not a real man at all – you're only a kind of … a kind of …

DANNY: A kind of what?

DARACH: I'm just trying to think of the word.

DANNY: You're not usually lost for words.

DARACH: A kind of a mixed up (*pause*) mongrel. An auld stray.

DANNY (*Angry*): Fuck off, you cunt!

DARACH: Oh, I'm not usually lost for words, you're saying, and when I find the right words, you don't like them. Sure maybe you go for men too – a queer – that'd be you alright.

DANNY: And so what if I did!

DARACH: You probably do … sure you're only a kind of a shadow of a man, a ghost of a man who still hasn't found out what men is supposed to do … real men.

DANNY: You fuck off for yourself! I never raped anybody! (DARACH *explodes. He goes for Danny*).

DARACH: Look it now, you fucker. You dirty, liardy cunt ya! You're like the rest of them. (*There is a scuffle and* DARACH *grabs him by the neck and pins him against the wall*). Are you accusing me, are you? (*Danny is speechless*). Cause I'll split your skull against that range so I will. (DARACH *loosens his grip somewhat*).

DANNY: I'm not accusing you of nothing. But it wouldn't have gone to court –

DARACH: They could prove nothing in court cause that case fell apart after two days, because it shouldn't have been held in the first place. (*Pause*). Sure the dogs in the street know that that's what England was like at the time, that they had in for every Irishman – all he had to do was to fart in the wrong place ... You keep your gob shut, I'm warning you.

DANNY: I'm saying nothing.

DARACH: Keep your trap shut so, if you're not. (*Pause. DARACH loosens his grip and they separate. Both fairly shaken*). And anyways, if I was guilty, wouldn't they have put me in jail.

DANNY: Not necessarily, when there's no justice in the law. Weren't the Guilford Four and the Birmingham Six put away, and they were innocent.

DARACH: They were.

DANNY: There's plenty of guilty people was never found guilty.

DARACH: Still roaming the streets, is it?

DANNY: Yeah, or they're prisoners of their own lives.

DARACH (*Banging his fist on the table*): Look it, are you trying to talk about me or are you talking about yourself? (*Goes to his room. Lights suddenly go to black*).

Kitchen/sitting room the following night. Darach is standing in the open door, back turned to the audience and looking into the distance. Glances at his watch. Stands in the door again, shoulder against the door-post.

DARACH: Well, would you look at your one coming down the road ... the state of her. By Christ, *a mhac*, ahh! You'd think she owned the place. (*Pause*). Oh, she's coming in. She doesn't seem to be bringing any flowers tonight ... sure maybe she saw where the ones she brought the last night ended up when she passed the grotto ... We'll have a bit of *craic* now ... (*Walks around the house rubbing his hands and stands behind the door until Cynthia arrives*). Ah, *muise*, come in, you're welcome, Cynthia *a ghrá*. (*Cynthia gets a fright at first and is surprised by his affected sweetness*). I heard you had a big date tonight. Oh sure, easily known and the get-up of you. (*Cynthia stands by the door, ill at ease, and not sure whether she should sit down or remain standing*).

CYNTHIA: Is he in?

DARACH: Coleman, is it? He's in alright, though I'd say out for count is more like it. He's back in the room, snoring away.

CYNTHIA: Danny!

DARACH: He went to bed early. Tired he was. You know yourself the way it is with old people, not dead yet; staying alive, like.

CYNTHIA: Danny, I said!

DARACH: Oh, I'm sorry Cynthia; sorry; Danny was it you wanted? Well, if he's here, I can't see him. Can you see him, Cynthia? (*Looks around and under the table*).

CYNTHIA: Is he up in his room?

DARACH: Well, the way it is, Cynthia, you see, I'm not allowed into Daniel's room, so I couldn't tell you what's in the room and what's not in it. Privacy, you understand. Our Danny boy is a fierce private person.

CYNTHIA: Well, is he in or is he out?

DARACH: Well, Cynthia, I'm sorry but I can't answer that question. I'd say God himself would be pushed to answer that one … You see, there's somebody up in that room all right, but do you know what, and this is the gospel truth, I don't know if it's a man or a woman. (*Pause*). When I was over there at the head of the stairs, I thought I saw a bit of a skirt rising up, so I'm kind of confused … unless maybe he has other women in here – a bit on the side, as they say … or maybe the fairies took him away and left a changeling in his place.

CYNTHIA: Nonsense!

DARACH: Oh, I'll tell you, it's no nonsense. There's such a thing as fairies you know. And you can trust no-one in this world. Not even our Danny. (*Cynthia is completely confused*). Were ye supposed to go out tonight or something?

CYNTHIA (*Assertively*): We are going out tonight. Getting out of this bloody place, not that it's any of your business what we do.

DARACH: Oh, I doubt if you are, Cynthia, cause I think Daniel has changed his plans. A lot went on here the last night. I'd say it's a case of Plan B or Plan C tonight. I heard him telling Maggie he wouldn't be needing her to baby-sit the auld fella tonight.

CYNTHIA (*Incredulous*): Rubbish.

DARACH: Oh, I heard him saying himself that he couldn't go out.

CYNTHIA: Why not?

DARACH (*In woman's voice*): Oh, I have nothing to wear, he said. (*Shrugs his shoulders in feminine fashion*).

CYNTHIA: Rubbish. (*Heading for the stairs*).

DARACH: Careful! (*Stops her. Stands in her way*). Don't frighten him. He might be in the middle of some job, downloading women from the internet or something. He told me that if you came in, to tell you not to go up to his room, on your life, until he had cleared the place up ... I think he's getting ready for a fashion show or something and he was talking of going modelling, believe it or not. On the catwalk. (*Pause*). But I should say nothing – in case I let the cat out of the bag (*Pause*). I think he wanted to surprise you and I wouldn't like to ruin the occasion. (*Whispering*). It's a secret, you see? Personal, like. Our Danny has any amount of them. Private affairs. When the cat's away, the mice are at play. Sure the auld fella doesn't even know about it, and himself and Danny Boy are very great. (*Cynthia is getting worried, as if realising that there is some truth in what he says*). I'm going out, Cynthia. I'm going down to JJ's to watch Sky Sports. Man. United are playing tonight – playing some team from Spain or Greece or somewhere and I'd like to see them being thrashed. I hope they get the shite beaten out of them. (*Takes a knife off the table and throws it up against Danny's door*). Danny! Daniel! Is there anybody home? If there is, could she or he come out. It's time to give in. (*Laughs*). The army has landed. (*Goes out the door whistling 'Danny Boy'. He has disappeared by the time* DANNY *comes out looking a bit shook*).

DANNY: Oh, Cynthia, Cynthia! It's yourself. I didn't hear you coming.

CYNTHIA (*Fidgety*): It was Darach. Darach threw the knife. He was at the door when I came in and I couldn't ring the doorbell.

DANNY: Alright. Alright. (*Still at the head of the stairs. Cynthia downstairs all this time and surprised that he hasn't come down*).

CYNTHIA: What's wrong with Darach tonight? He was being really odd. Well, odder than he usually is.

DANNY: Good question.

CYNTHIA: What do you mean?

DANNY: Did he say much?

CYNTHIA: He was blathering and gig-acting there for the last ten minutes, but I couldn't make head nor tail out of what he was saying.

DANNY: Cynthia.

CYNTHIA: Yea?

DANNY (*Affectionately*): Come here.

CYNTHIA: What?

DANNY: Come up here. (*Cynthia excited and worried at once*).

CYNTHIA: What's going on, Danny?

DANNY: I have to warn you, Cynthia. You'll be shocked.

CYNTHIA: Danny! I hope there's no skeletons up there, is there? (*Laughing*).

DANNY (*Seriously*): I'm very sorry for leaving it so long, Cynthia. I've been putting this day off for years, and I hope you forgive me.

CYNTHIA: It's alright, Danny, it's alright. I'd forgive you anything. (*She's very excited going upstairs*). Wow. I'm ready. I'm ready. I can't believe it. How about … how about December, maybe. Christmastime would be nice. We'll have to give the priest three months' notice anyways, like.

DANNY: Steady on, steady on. Hold your horses, Cynthia. (DANNY *turns on the light. They go into the bedroom.* CYNTHIA *looks around. There are a couple of dresses hanging from the walls, underwear and various articles of women's clothing sticking out of boxes which have been left on the bed. Also a couple of ladies' hats*).

CYNTHIA (*Confused*): What is this? For a play?

DANNY: No. No. Let me explain.

CYNTHIA (*Taking down one of the dresses*): For me? (*Pause*). But I never wear orange. You know I …

DANNY: Hold on.

CYNTHIA: Is there somebody else? (*Moving away from Danny*). Darach said that …

DANNY: No! And it doesn't matter what Darach says. I love you, Cynthia, and no-one else but you and I've always been faithful to you.

CYNTHIA: Well, that's what I thought but –

DANNY: But there's something about me that I have to tell you. I'm not going to beat around the bush any longer. (*Shaking*). Trans. (*Pause*). I'm a transvestite (*Pause*).

CYNTHIA: What? (*Shocked and speechless*).

DANNY: Trans (*Stops*). I'm sorry – but that the beginning and the end of it to put it bluntly. I can't help it. That's the way I am, Cynthia. That's the way I'll always be.

CYNTHIA: Danny! (*Appalled. Stares wide-eyed at the clothes. Distraught. Unable to speak and unable to absorb what she has just heard*). Danny!

DANNY: I'm sorry, Cynthia. Like I said …

CYNTHIA: But that couldn't be true.

DANNY: It could, Cynthia, and it is.

CYNTHIA: But Danny, Danny! (*Flops down on the bed. DANNY goes over to her and is about to put his arm around her. She pushes him away*). Stay away from me!

DANNY: Cynthia, I'm sorry –

CYNTHIA (*Sharply*): I heard you. I'm not deaf. (*Prolonged uncomfortable pause*).

DANNY: I'm sorry.

CYNTHIA: I don't understand. Playing games.

DANNY: They're no games. It's my life –

CYNTHIA: Stop it. Stop it, I tell you! (*Puts her hand on her tummy. Bursts into tears. Pause. Lifts her head after a while. Starts examining the clothes in the box. Stops suddenly when she spots a particular item. Stands up and picks up the panties and the bra*). They're mine ! My – (*Danny is rather embarrassed*). You stole them off our line. And I had a huge row with my sister over them.

DANNY: When I saw –

CYNTHIA: Buying them for me so you could wear them yourself. That's some birthday present! (*Stamps her foot*). (*Prolonged pause. Cynthia still crying. Sits down again*).

DANNY (*Calmly*): I know this is hard for you, Cynthia. They're only clothes, rags, made out of cotton, wool, silk … I'm the same person, Cynthia, so I am and I still love you the same inside these clothes. Well you know what they say … put silk on a goat (*Laughs, trying to ease the tension*).

CYNTHIA (*Enraged*): Put silk on a goat. Rubbish! The goat in the temple, more like it!

DANNY: I don't know what you mean, Cynthia.

CYNTHIA: That doesn't matter, cause I don't understand you, yourself and your secrets.

DANNY: But –

CYNTHIA: I don't know you any more, Danny. And you're making a fool of me.

DANNY: Cynthia! No-one is making a fool of anyone. You don't understand –

CYNTHIA (*Screaming*): If you tell me once more that I don't understand! I know fecking well that I don't fecking understand. But I do know you're making an eejit out of me.

DANNY: I wasn't making an eejit out of you. I was going to tell you –

CYNTHIA (*Raging*): Yeah right! On our wedding day, was it. When we'd go back to the hotel to change our clothes on our honeymoon, is it. When you'd take off your trousers and when I see you wearing a pair of knickers … that's when you'd tell me, is it?

DANNY: Cynthia (*Moving towards her. CYNTHIA turns her back to him and he stands still*).

CYNTHIA: And me coming up here. (*Pause*). Sure that you were going to propose.

DANNY: And why wouldn't we get married?

CYNTHIA: So that I'd be married to … to … to a (*pause*) … to a freak. So that I'd be stuck with him. So that he'd be wearing his trousers today and a my frock tomorrow, is that it?

DANNY: That's not it. If you only let me explain.

CYNTHIA: There's nothing to explain (*Looks around at the clothes*).

DANNY: I'm sorry, Cynthia. If you only understood –

CYNTHIA: Don't mention understanding to me, I'm telling you! Yourself and your room make me sick. (DANNY *sits down, knowing that there's no point trying to explain the situation.* CYNTHIA *going round in circles as though dizzy. Suddenly, she breaks down crying and runs out of the room, downstairs and out the door, leaving the door open*). Freak! Freak!

DANNY (*Running after her*): Cynthia! Cynthia! Hold on! (*Glances at the door of Coleman's room, afraid he has woken him. Closes the front door. Looks around the house*). Oh Christ! (*Goes upstairs, slowly, and goes into his room. Looks at the clothes in front of him. Sighs. Looks at himself in the mirror as if disgusted with himself or hoping to find someone else. Throws himself on his bed*).

Our Lady's Grotto an hour later. (Use corner of the stage). One spotlight. A large bright statue can be seen, stones around it. With the lights we see Cynthia who has obviously been crying, her eyes still wet. She is not praying, she is sitting with her back to the statues. Someone is heard approaching. CYNTHIA wipes the tears from her eyes and tries to pull herself together. MAGGIE enters carrying a bunch of flowers.

MAGGIE: O, Cynthia! I didn't recognise you there at first. What are you –

CYNTHIA: Nothing. I was just – (*Maggie realises that all is not well*).

MAGGIE: Ah Cynthia, you were crying. And you shouldn't be out in the cold.

CYNTHIA: I was only … I wanted to be alone.

MADDIE: O, I'm sorry Cynthia. I only came with some fresh flowers for the grotto and to light a little candle.

CYNTHIA: I know.

MAGGIE: I try and spend a few minutes with our Lady every day. She's our Mother of Perpetual Help, you know? You can put your faith in her.

CYNTHIA (*About to leave*): Our Mother of Perpetual Help … Nana used to talk about her.

MAGGIE: O, stay where you are, stay where you are, Cynthia *a ghrá*. Don't let me be hunting you. This grotto is for everybody. It's especially for those who are anxious or worried. I'll be off now as soon as I light this candle. (*Pause. Slightly curious*). Is it Danny, is it? O, I'm sorry, *a ghrá* – I shouldn't be asking.

CYNTHIA: Yeah, it's Danny alright.

MAGGIE: Ah, I understand. There'll always be problems with these things. They're never easy, or as simple as they might seem. (*Cynthia starts crying again*). Ssh. Now now Cynthia.

(*Puts a hand on her shoulder*). Things will be alright again in a day or two. All couples have the odd hitch.

CYNTHIA: I don't know.

MAGGIE: Ara they will, *a ghrá*. Love is patient, you see.

CYNTHIA: Ah?

MAGGIE: You're thinking now that an auld one like myself would know nothing about love, Cynthia, an auld codger like me that never got married.

CYNTHIA: I'm not.

MAGGIE: I was engaged once you know. Would you believe that? (*Trying to lift her spirits*).

CYNTHIA: Engaged … to be married!

MAGGIE: What else? (*Pause*). And sure you don't even need to ask who it was. (*Pause*). Sure it was Coleman, the creature.

CYNTHIA: Coleman!

MAGGIE: It was; Coleman. Indeed 'n' it was. There's not many now would know that. Well, I suppose some of the older ones would know right enough. Even Danny and Darach, I doubt if they know.

CYNTHIA: And … and …

MAGGIE: And what happened, is it. Aren't you the nosy one! Well, I did something stupid. I broke it off cause I got cold feet or something. I don't know what hit me, but I finished it. I made a mistake. I made a mistake, Cynthia, if it was a mistake. You never know where your luck lies.

CYNTHIA: Imagine! I knew nothing about that.

MAGGIE: But Coleman got over it, thank God, and he married my best friend Kate and I was glad … glad for both of them. Well I was until that cursed thunder came. (CYNTHIA *laughs gently. Pause*).

CYNTHIA: I was just trying to imagine yourself and Coleman married.

MAGGIE: Some things are best left to the imagination, loveen. (*Pause*). That includes marriages too sometimes. You never know. (*Pause*). And in a funny way, weren't we together in the end. Myself and Coleman. Isn't it funny the way thing happen. (*Pause*). You light that candle there and leave your worries with the Blessed Virgin. (*Cynthia trembling slightly*). No, hold on, I'll light it for you, for your intention – if you hold this vase for me. (*Cynthia holds on to the vase*). Ah, Danny is a nice fella, Cynthia. He'll look after you, so he will. Did you know I'm his godmother? And I'm Darach's godmother too. Darach is not a bad fella either, though you might think otherwise from the way he carries on. He does be acting the hard man, but a lot of that is only put on. And sure, I'd know because you could say I half-reared them. Darach was very put out by his mother's death – more than any of the others. He took it very bad. That's our Darach. (*Cynthia bursts out crying*). O, I'm sorry, Cynthia, loveen, I'm sorry. I forgot. (*Pause. She takes the lighted candle from Cynthia in case she drops it. CYNTHIA hurries away. MAGGIE turns to face the statue and is about to place the candle in the grotto*). O, Mother of God. Holy Mother of God.

Sitting room/kitchen. Late that night/early the next morning. Danny is at the top of the stairs in the darkness/half-light. He's wearing his mother's dress and a wig. Comes downstairs slowly, carefully, reflecting. Goes to the telephone. Dials a number and sits down.

DANNY: Hi Cynthia. Cynthia, it's Danny here. I suspected you'd have the phone turned off, or that you wouldn't answer it. I can't sleep. I feel funny … well I suppose funny's not the right word for it. (*Pause*). In a way I'm glad you have the phone turned off because this way I'll be able to finish what I have to say without you interrupting me. And sure even if you were never to listen to it, I'll have got it off my chest. (*Pause*). I'm sorry, Cynthia, about what happened. I should have been honest with you and told you straight out the way things were. But there's some things that are hard to say out straight. (*Pause*). Especially in Connemara. (*Laughs slightly*). Anywhere I suppose, cause Connemara isn't the most remote part of the country any more. But like I was saying, or like I tried to say tonight … it's as if there was somebody else inside of me … (*Pause. Bleep. Phone cuts off*). Flip! (*Dials number once more and waits for the machine to click in*). Cynthia. It's me again. The machine cut me off. But anyways, as I was saying (*Pause*). It's as if there was somebody else inside of me, somebody that can't sit still a lot of the time. (*Pause*). Other times then I know well it's me that's in it or else another version of me. Or maybe it's how I don't let out the stranger inside me, so that I could be at home with myself, at ease, like. That's why I sometimes wear women's clothes. It's as if I have this craving – a mad passion or urge – inside of me that I have to satisfy. It's as if I have no choice. That I have to give in or go out of my mind. Out of my mind. (*Pause*). I'd go cracked. This urge, it's got a grip of me. (*Pause*). I hope you understand, Cynthia. (*Pause*). I hope you understand I'm trying to explain things to you and that I still love you. You might ring me tomorrow. Good night now, love. (*Puts down the phone. Sits there. Lights fade on him as he sits in his chair*).

Sitting room/kitchen. An hour or two later. Darkness. Then thunder and lightening. We see Danny in his chair. He wakes up but then remains seated, like a statue. COLEMAN comes out of his bedroom wearing only pyjamas and holding a Tellytubby. Danny doesn't move. Lights quite low for this scene.

COLEMAN: Where's the holy water? The holy water. (*Goes to one of the presses and takes out a bottle. Takes the lid off and blesses himself. Shakes a few drops around the house and into his room*). Darach. Holy water. (*Goes to Darach's room and shakes a few drops of holy water into the room. Closes the door again*). Danny. A drop of holy water. (*Goes over towards the stairs and goes up a step of two and shakes the water upwards*). Holy water, Danny. To protect you from the thunder. (*Turns to come down again and sees Danny sitting down, staring out before him, still wearing his mother's dress and a wig. He thinks it's Kate*). Kate. Kate. It's yourself, God bless you. I knew well you'd not leave me on my own a night like tonight. Kate. Kate. (*Hugs Danny. DANNY is taken aback but plays along and lets Coleman think he is Kate*). I hope the thunder won't wake the children. Move in towards the range, it's cold over there at the window. I don't like that thunder, Kate. I don't like it one bit, you know. It keeps me awake. (*They head over towards the chair. DANNY remains standing*). I'll sit down here a whileen. Throw me over the *Watchtower*. It's over there on the table. You go back to bed, if you're tired, like a good woman. The kids have you worn out. (DANNY *hands him his* Watchtower). I'll follow you in a minute, as soon as the thunder stops. (*He sits down. DANNY opens the door to Coleman's room but doesn't go in and closes it. Stands behind Coleman whose head bows and who starts bobbing off to sleep. When Danny is satisfied that Coleman is dozing, he opens the bedroom door again without waking him, leaves it open and goes up to his own room. The audience cannot see him in his own room. Very heavy rain, thunder and lightening can be heard.* COLEMAN *sits up. The bedroom door is open. Silence. Day is breaking*).

COLEMAN (*speaking back into the room*): There's nobody here, Kate. There's nobody here. The children mustn't have got up yet. We'd better not wake them, Kate. We'd better let them sleep. Since there's no school today. (*He has a copy of* Watchtower *in one hand and a* Tellytubby *in the other*). Jehovah. (*Opens the magazine. Reads*). 'Life after Death'. Christ, the print is awful small in this bloody book and I can't find my magnifying glass wherever I put it ... There's not many pockets in pyjamas. Ah, sure, maybe it's not worth reading. (*Pause*). What do you think, Kate? (*Looks over at the room*). I wonder should we join the Jehovahs, the two of us, like. (*Laughs a little*). The two of us, together. (*Pause. As if he's waiting for her to reply*). I don't know, by dad. (*Pause*). That's what we should do by rights – we'll ask the priest after Mass so – later on. We will, by dad. He'd know. And if the priest says it's all right, we'll join up. We will, so we will, by dad. (*Pause*). Do you think, Kate? I suppose you might be right, that you're better off being in with them all, with the lot of them ... There's a lot of them out there – there is surely. (*Pause*). The Muslims. They're there all right. But they do be throwing stones at each other. Well they do be throwing stones at women anyways and you wouldn't like that, Kate. And you'd be right. They must have plenty of stones over there where they're from. Any amount of them. (*Pause*). No more than Connemara. They'll never see the end of the stones, so, if that's how it is. They won't. (*Pause*). And there's others. (*Pause*). But then some of them do be flaking each other, don't they. The Hindus killing the Muslims ... or Jesus, maybe it's the Muslims do be killing the Buddhists, if I'm not getting them mixed up, and Christ, that carry on is no good either ... killing people because they have a different religion ... like the Catholics and the Protestants up North, is it. Well, it is and it isn't, Kate. The Catholics and the Protestants do be killing each other right enough, but that's different like. (*Pause. Lights lower slightly. Talking to the Tellytubby*). But what's this Darach said about the Jehovahs ... that they wouldn't let me gamble or go out to bingo or put in for the raffle ... but sure, what's the point of living if you have to live without them things ... no point, I'll tell you. (*Glances at* Watchtower). *Watchtower!* But sure I suppose we might be able to sneak out to bingo every Wednesday unknowns to them ... like we used to sneak out to the dances long ago, Kate, unknowns to the priests – themselves and their blackthorn sticks. But he mentioned blood too so he did. (*Pause*). If you were needing blood ... If you were needing a blood transfusion. Sure if Galway Bay was full of blood and you up to your neck in it ... they wouldn't give you a drop of it. Not a drop of blood would they give you ... Not a thimbleful ... even if the sky turned to blood ... And do you know what, I don't think I'd mind. I don't think I would. I'd do without blood, any day of the week ... I would, you know, but bingo now on a Wednesday night ... and the raffle ... and the horses ... where would I be without them? Where would I be without them? (*Pause. The* Watchtower *falls out of his hand to the floor. His head rolls back gently. The Tellytubby falls from his hand onto his chest. His arms fall down by his side*).

Kitchen/sitting room. Day after the funeral. It is morning. Danny has more or less finished packing and is ready to go. He is tidying the kitchen and every so often picks out something which belongs to him and throws it into his bag. The house looks emptier than before. The door to Coleman's room is open. Maggie is there, standing by the door, as if feeling slightly out of place.

DANNY (*To himself*): It's hard to think of everything.

MAGGIE: If you want me to look after anything …

DANNY: I don't, Maggie. (*Looks at his watch*). I think everything is sorted at this stage. But thanks for all your help.

MAGGIE: It was the least I could do.

DANNY: Especially the day of the funeral. Only for you … (*Pause*).

MAGGIE (*Lump in her throat*): I'll miss him. Coleman the creature. I'll sorely miss him.

DANNY: I know that, Maggie. And we all appreciate the way you looked after him. Sure you were like a mother to him.

MAGGIE: Like a wife. (*Laughs*). Nearly!

DANNY: Like a wife and a mother, so. Either which way, you couldn't have done more for him.

MAGGIE: I only did my best. Maybe that's what happens. (*Pause*).

DANNY: What do you mean, what happens?

MAGGIE: When people don't get married.

DANNY: I suppose, sometimes.

MAGGIE: They look after other peoples' people? (*Lump in her throat*). When they have none of their own.

DANNY: Well, some of them anyways.

MAGGIE: Danny. (*Pause*). I don't know what I'll do from now on. (*She starts to cry*).

DANNY (*Going over to her*): Ah, Maggie.

MAGGIE: I'm sorry, Danny, to be like this the day you're going and everything like, but I was part of the family too, you know, for the last twenty-five years. (*Pause*). And today is Wednesday. (*Pause*). And Coleman, the creature.

DANNY: Ah now, now, Maggie.

MAGGIE: Every Wednesday. Every bingo night. Any night I could, I'd come over here to look after him, the creature, and indeed, it was easy to look after him. I don't know how I'm going to pass those nights from now on. (*Pause*). Over there inside the walls of my own house.

DANNY: But won't the bingo still be there, Maggie?

MAGGIE: No. No, it won't be the same. My life is over without Coleman. I might as well – I might as well be –

DANNY: Ah now, Maggie. (DARACH *comes in the front door. He's wearing old clothes himself and is taking old clothes and bits and pieces from Coleman's room and burning them*).

DARACH: O, there you are Maggie. If you have anything for burning, now's your chance. (*Heads for Coleman's room*). I'm building a bonfire with this auld rubbish. (*From the room. Grabs old underpants, blankets, clothes, a Wellington boot and a plastic flower-pot*). This is a full-time job you know, and there should be a health warning with it. (*Exits*). (MAGGIE *shrugs her shoulders*).

MAGGIE: There won't be much of me seen around this house any more, Danny. (*Looks around*). Except when you're coming home yourself. If you are going to be coming home. (*Pause*). Will you be coming home?

DANNY (*Takes deep breath*): I don't know, Maggie. From time to time maybe. (*Pause*). Maybe I mightn't. I don't know what's in store for me.

MAGGIE: For a visit.

DANNY: For a visit.

MAGGIE: I wouldn't blame you if you didn't come back to live here. Ye'll have more peace over there.

DANNY: We? (*Slips out*).

MAGGIE: Yourself and Cynthia. (*Questioning*). Of course, that's what I was talking about. (*Laughs*) You hardly thought I meant yourself and Darach. (*Lowers her voice*). You'd have peace nowhere with that fella.

DANNY: Well that's true. Is it getting away from him, I am. And now is my chance. Lord have mercy on the auld fella. But I can do whatever I like now.

MAGGIE: Hah? (*Knock on the door. CYNTHIA enters*).

MAGGIE: O, I was just leaving. (*Putting on her coat*).

DANNY: We'll not be rushing ya, Maggie.

MAGGIE: Ah, well ye have arrangements to be making. (*Smiles over at Cynthia*). I only came in to say bye-bye to Danny and I might as well say goodbye to you, Cynthia, in case I don't see you. (*Gives Cynthia a hug, who looks distinctly uncomfortable. Then shakes hands with Danny. DARACH enters to collect more material*).

DARACH: Ah, Cynthia, if ye have anything up there for burning. Old clothes, like. We'll be having a bonfire out here shortly. (*Goes back into the room*).

CYNTHIA: I don't think so, somehow. (*Short, slightly awkward pause, as though they are all waiting for Darach to leave again. He comes out the room with a black bag, an old pair of slippers, a Tellytubby and a few odds and ends besides*).

MAGGIE: You'll ring me now, when you land, won't you Danny? Just to let me know you're landed.

DANNY: I will, of course, Maggie. I'll ring you – as sure as I'm standing here, I will.

DARACH: As sure as you'll be standing there, more like it.

DANNY: It doesn't make any difference.

DARACH: Well, do you know, it *does* make a difference. Sure you can't be ringing her from there if you're standing here. (*Pause*). Anyways, Maggie, sure the plane might fall out of the sky. They're dropping like flies these days. And if it goes down over the sea sure you'll be neither here nor there.

MAGGIE: Danny has a mobile phone now.

DARACH: Ah, but you can't use them on planes. Interference, you understand ... Interference. (*Darach exits*).

DANNY: Never mind him.

MAGGIE (*Blessing herself*): Oh, Mother of God, but I never had any time for those planes. There isn't a week goes by but one of them falls out of the sky – sometimes two of them. It's true for me. (*Slightly shaken*). And they fly so high. I don't know why they go up so far. What if somebody planted a bomb on one of them? (DARACH *comes in and takes a box of matches off the table. Shakes it to make sure there's something in it*). It said in the paper that the Taliban were coming to Ireland.

DARACH: The Taliban! Didn't they land last night. (*Pause*). Back in Lettermullen. It won't be long now before they're here. (DARACH *exits*).

DANNY: Oh, Maggie. Those planes are perfectly safe. Sure you were never in a plane.

MAGGIE: I wasn't and I won't be in one. Even if I was dead, I wouldn't set foot in one. (*Pause*). Well, I'm losing the run of myself now, maybe. I'll say goodbye to ye so. (*Hugs Danny*). And I'll say a prayer for ye at the grotto on my way back home. (MAGGIE *exits. Pause*).

DANNY: Poor auld Maggie is in a bad way.

CYNTHIA: She is. (*Pause*). I didn't come here to talk about Maggie.

DANNY: So much happened this week and –

CYNTHIA: I know you had a rough week with your father's death and all the rest.

DANNY: Sing it to me sister ... especially all the rest.

CYNTHIA: So?

DANNY: So? (*Pause. A fire can be heard cracking outside. Vibrant flames can be seen through the window – as though the clothes etc have been doused with oil. They are briefly distracted by the fire. Fire burns throughout remainder of the scene*).

CYNTHIA: So (*Sternly*). You're off then. London, I hear.

DANNY: Yep.

CYNTHIA: Yep. Just like that.

DANNY: There's nothing to keep me here.

CYNTHIA: Nothing!

DANNY: What is there? In Connemara. There's nothing here.

CYNTHIA: So I'm nothing now, am I?

DANNY: That's not what I mean, Cynthia, and you know it's not.

CYNTHIA (*Sarcastically*): You wanted to marry me a week ago.

DANNY: I did, yeah. So?

CYNTHIA: So?

DANNY: You said you wouldn't marry me. (*Lowers his voice*). You said I was a freak.

CYNTHIA: It all came kinda sudden. What if I changed my mind after a while? When I had thawed out a little and could accept you as you are.

DANNY: As if … (*Indifferent*)

CYNTHIA: Now that Coleman is dead, all you want is to go. You don't care about me. You never did.

DANNY: I've made up my mind about this and I've made arrangements. What's over is over.

CYNTHIA: That's the way you see it, is it? You could have told me that you were going, instead of me hearing it doing the rounds in the pub.

DANNY: You wouldn't listen to me when I wanted to speak to you. (*Pause*). That's the way it is and there's no going back now.

CYNTHIA: Do you not feel anything? Anything at all for the three years we spent together?

DANNY: Life goes on. I had no choice. You come and you go.

CYNTHIA: And that's all it means to you. Look at me, Danny! You never really loved me, did you?

DANNY: Sure weren't we engaged?

CYNTHIA: That's not the question I asked you!

DANNY: What question? (*Pause*). If I really loved you?

CYNTHIA: Do you want me to give you a definition of what love is? Don't be playing dumb, Danny!

DANNY (*Angry*): I did love you, but you lay down your own conditions. Real love is unconditional, in case you've never heard so before.

CYNTHIA: You weren't honest with me.

DANNY: I wasn't the one who finished things. Who walked. I was willing to get married.

CYNTHIA (*Sarcastically, emphatically*): You were, were you? (*Angrily*). Yeah, right, some time in the future. You were, when it came to the crunch ... or at least until you could come up with your latest excuse.

DANNY: Now, now.

CYNTHIA: And you let me put my trust in you. Share my love and all my other emotions with you. Waste years of my life on you. Years of my life wasted. And you used me. You used me like you'd use a toy.

DANNY: Cynthia! I didn't use you.

CYNTHIA: You never really loved me, did you. You were just using me. (*Fire crackles outside*).

DANNY: If that's the case there were two of us in it. (CYNTHIA *loses the head*).

CYNTHIA: Two of us! So you're admitting it. There were two of us, while you were waiting for Coleman to die –

DANNY: Nonsense!

CYNTHIA: Until you were free to do whatever you liked. So that you could go off, and I could go to hell.

DANNY: That's how you see it.

CYNTHIA: That's how it is.

DANNY: Fuck it! Life is one big fucking mess. It is, you know –

CYNTHIA: It's not. It is not! Your life is going according to plan. Only my life is a mess. (*Crying*). But it's some consolation knowing that you are aware of the mess you and your lies have made of my life, though it doesn't change the fact that you've been ruining my life for the past three liardy years. Traitor! Traitor! (*She runs out the door.* DANNY *looks out the door, but says nothing. He is in shock. Standing there motionless. Looks around the room as though dumbfounded. Gathers his thoughts, walks around the room. Looks out the window at the dancing flames*).

DANNY: That's that, then. (*Looks around to see if he has left anything behind. Occasionally picks something up and puts it in the top of his bag. Looks at the door of Darach's room. Goes over to the door of Coleman's room and enters. Comes out, leaving the door open after him, looking at the Tellytubby he's holding. Takes a deep breath and puts the toy into his bag. Looks around once more. Glances upstairs towards his room. Goes up slowly. Opens the door. Goes into the room and turns on the light. The room has been cleaned out, and is practically empty, though the bed has not been stripped and there is a picture of Cynthia on the dressing table. He looks around the room, with affection and with some sadness. Sits on his bed. Bows his head again*). That's that, then. (*He stands up. Looks at himself in the long mirror. Then pushes it aside. Looks around, takes the lone photograph of Cynthia from the dressing table and looks at it carefully*). Lies, freak, traitor. (*Pause*). That's what she said. (*Throws it into the waste basket. Goes over to one of the cupboards. Opens the door and puts his arm into the press as if feeling something inside. Overcome by emotion. Closes the cupboard door while staring into it. Goes to the bedroom door. Gives one last look around the room. Turns off the light. Closes the door after him. Stands for a minute at the top of the stairs, thinking. Opens the door again. Turns on the light. Pointedly leaves the door open and walks downstairs. Looks at his watch.* DARACH *enters and stands in the doorway. Danny is at the foot of the stairs at this point*). I'm hitting the road, as soon as the taxi comes.

DARACH: Well, you know where the door is.

DANNY: Ha?

DARACH: I said, you know where the door is, if you're leaving.

DANNY: That's a nice way of saying goodbye to your brother.

DARACH: Is it any worse than pretending?

DANNY: I hope you'll be alright here on your own.

DARACH: What's be wrong with me, here on my own.

DANNY: Nothing, I suppose.

DARACH: Exactly – nothing. I'll have a bit of peace.

DANNY: You will. Any amount of it.

DARACH: Peace – and a break from cracked people.

DANNY: Cracked people?

DARACH: Yeah. Cracked people and nutcases. You with your rags and your robes. The auld fella and his vertigo. Maggie with her coupons and the Virgin Mary. Cynthia and her ... her –

DANNY: Her what?

DARACH: Ah, I don't know. (*Pause*). Is she going with you, or is she following you?

DANNY: Is it any concern of yours – no more than the other business?

DARACH: It isn't. (*Pause*). I suppose.

DANNY: Well, since you asked, she's neither coming with me nor following me.

DARACH (*Surprised, softly*): It makes no odds to me.

DANNY: It doesn't ... I suppose. And she won't be coming here either to annoy you when I'm not around. (*Pause*).

DARACH: Why should she?

DANNY: Because you never did a charitable thing or a Christian deed in your life – for her or for any one else – only doing wrong by people.

DARACH (*Angry*): Doing wrong by people. After two thousand years of Christianity, if you can call it Christianity, there's plenty of wrong being done, and I should know; believe me I should know. And if you give it another two thousand years your so-called Christians will still be doing the same thing.

DANNY: Well, you've done you're share, that's for sure.

DARACH: Would ya look at who's talking. (*Pause*). Look it, Danny, *a mhac*. There's people mightn't like me cause I say what I mean, cause I don't go in for *plámásing*. But I don't cod people. At least they know where they stand. I can say that much.

DANNY: Look it, Darach. At the end of the day, you're my brother (*pause*) my only brother, and I might never see you again. It's for your own sake I am. We might never have seen eye to eye, but I don't like to see anyone going down the wrong road.

DARACH: Would you listen to him! He's going to give a sermon – good on ya!

DANNY: I'm only telling you to make something of your life, to be more understanding, and to have more respect for people. If you don't, you'll end up like a prisoner – in solitary confinement in this house.

DARACH: A prisoner, if you don't mind, and I having done nothing to nobody. Like the Birmingham Six is it or the Guilford Four maybe?

DANNY: Kind of!

DARACH: Kind of! And sure I can walk out of here any time I like. (*Raises his arms*). Knock the walls down if I feel like it? Heh? Who can stop me? Isn't it true for me?

DANNY: It is.

DARACH: And if it is so.

DANNY: You can't just walk out of your life whenever you feel like it. That's what I mean. Because you can't see the wall that surrounds you ... As if you were tying yourself down.

DARACH: Tying myself down. Tying myself down, my arse. And what kind of a halter do you be putting on ... Ah ... Powder and lipstick and slips and knickers and ... don't you be talking to me about freedom. You'd think that room of yours was some kind of a lobster pot.

DANNY (*Angry, grabs one of his bags*): There's no point talking.

DARACH: No point whatsoever. (*Pause*). Have you cleared it out?

DANNY: I have. I'm finished with that room.

DARACH: And all your bits and your bobs before they go up in smoke with the auld fella's rags. (*Pause*).

DANNY: I – I – I have.

DARACH: Just as well. A house is no place for that kind of trash. (*Car horn sounds*).

DANNY: That'll be the taxi. I'll be off so. (*Pause. Horn sounds again, repeatedly*). See you, so. (*Pause. Darach has turned his back to him and doesn't answer. DANNY exits. Leaves door open after him. DARACH hesitates, then looks over at the door to make sure he has gone. Car is heard starting up and fading into the distance*).

DARACH: See ya. (DARACH *goes over to the window and looks out. Then he goes over to the door as if watching the car, stretches as he watches it fade into the distance. He then closes the door, quietly. Leans against the door and remains silent for a while. He looks unhappy. Goes over to the door to his own room and looks in. Goes to the door to Coleman's room and stands at the door looking in. Then looks upstairs and goes up slowly. Stands at the door as if afraid to enter. Then goes in quietly and looks around the room, and up and down. Sniffs the air a couple of times. Pulls a face. Walks around the room and sees the waste-paper basket and the picture. Takes the picture out of the basket. Looks at it. Pulls a wry face again and is about to let the picture frame drop into the basket but changes his mind and places it flat, photograph facing down, on the table*). Now, you won't have her either. (*Looks around the room as if looking for something that isn't there. Then stands in the middle of the room. Goes over to the cupboard and opens it. He appears to get a fright and steps back. Steps forward again after a while and puts his hand into the cupboard, carefully, affectionately. Takes out his mother's dress and becomes very emotional. Holds the dress close to him. Then starts walking down the stairs, slowly and carefully. The doorbell rings. He is taken aback. Some letters are thrown through the letterbox onto the floor. He carefully places the dress on the chair. Goes to the window and looks out before picking up the envelopes. Looks at them one by one).* Reps of the Deceased Coleman Ridge ... (*Opens the envelope and takes out the letter and some sample* in memoriam *cards.*) Oh, yes, indeed. Memorial cards. (*Pause*). JJ Lalors Ltd. (*Looks at the second envelope. It's a large envelope, which seems to contain a magazine*). Mr Danny Ridge. (*Looks carefully at the letter, then looks up towards Danny's room as if expecting Danny to appear. Leaves the envelope on the table*). Danny! There's a letter here for you. (*Pause. Looks up at the bedroom. Pause. Then looks at the envelope again, and tears it open. Takes out a catalogue*). Homeshopping ... (*Turns page*). Boutique. More rags. (*Bins the catalogue as if in anger*). Rubbish. (*Picks up the other letter*). Mr Coleman Ridge ... Personal. (*Turns the envelope over and back a few times. Looks at the door to Coleman's room*). Coleman, there's a letter here for you. (*Pause. Opens the envelope, nervously. Takes out the letter and looks at it and a female voice is heard narrating it).*

VOICE: Dear Mr. Ridge, Congratulations! You are the lucky First-Prize Winner in our monthly draw for September and are now the proud owner of a new exercise bike worth over €500. (*Pause*). Please contact me as soon as possible at the above number so that we can arrange delivery. Once again, congratulations, and wishing you many happy healthy years of cycling and exercise. Yours sincerely ...

(DARACH *leaves the letter on the table in front of him. Stares at the letter, sits down, placing his hands in front of him on the table. Looks over at the dress. Gets up slowly, goes over to the chair and takes the dress in his hands, gently. Goes over to the window and looks at the fire. Holds the dress out in front of him for a second as if thinking of burning it. Lights gradually fade. three spotlights remain – two bright ones on the open doors to Danny and Coleman's respective rooms, and an even brighter one which focuses on Darach. DARACH takes up the letter. He looks at it, makes a ball of it, and squeezes it in his fist. Holding the dress in his hands, he embraces it gently. He stares in front of him, almost shaking. Lights fade; spots on the bedroom doors fade completely until the only remaining light is on Darach. Then go to black*).

The End.

Production History

The Connemara Five was first published in Irish as *Cuigear Conamara* by Cló Iar-Chonnachta in 2003. It was performed as the centrepiece of An Taibhdhearc's 75th birthday celebrations in Galway and in Dublin in October 2003.

Also by Micheál Ó Conghaile

Sna Fir (novel)

Seachrán Jeaic Sheáin Johnny (novella)

An Fear Nach nDéanann Gáire (short fiction)

An Fear a Phléasc (short fiction)

Mac an tSagairt (short fiction)

Cúigear Chonamara (play)

Comhrá Caillí (poetry)

Gnéithe d'Amhráin Chonamara ár Linne (musicology)

Conamara agus Árainn 1880-1980 (history)

Sláinte: Deich mBliana de Chló Iar-Chonnachta (editor)

Gaeltacht Ráth Cairn: Léachtaí Comórtha (editor)

Croch Suas É! (editor)

Up Seanamhach (editor)

Fís agus Teanga (editor)

Ualach an Uaignis by Martin MacDonagh (translated into Irish)

Banríon Álainn an Líonáin by Martin MacDonagh (translated into Irish)

Fourfront (short fiction)

Published by Cló Iar-Chonnachta